FRANC
THE LADIES

Francis Vivian was bc
1906 at East Retford, Nottinghamshire. He was
the younger brother of noted photographer Hallam
Ashley. Vivian laboured for a decade as a painter
and decorator before becoming an author of popular
fiction in 1932. In 1940 he married schoolteacher
Dorothy Wallwork, and the couple had a daughter.

After the Second World War he became assistant
editor at the Nottinghamshire Free Press and circuit
lecturer on many subjects, ranging from crime to
bee-keeping (the latter forming a major theme in
the Inspector Knollis mystery *The Singing Masons*).
A founding member of the Nottingham Writers'
Club, Vivian once awarded first prize in a writing
competition to a young Alan Sillitoe, the future
bestselling author.

The ten Inspector Knollis mysteries were published
between 1941 and 1956. In the novels, ingenious
plotting and fair play are paramount. A colleague
recalled that 'the reader could always arrive at a
correct solution from the given data. Inspector
Knollis never picked up an undisclosed clue which,
it was later revealed, held the solution to the mystery
all along.'

Francis Vivian died on April 2, 1979 at the age of 73.

THE INSPECTOR KNOLLIS MYSTERIES
Available from Dean Street Press

FRANCIS VIVIAN

THE LADIES OF LOCKSLEY

With an introduction by Curtis Evans

DEAN STREET PRESS

INTRODUCTION

SHORTLY BEFORE his death in 1951, American agriculturalist and scholar Everett Franklin Phillips, then Professor Emeritus of Apiculture (beekeeping) at Cornell University, wrote British newspaperman Arthur Ernest Ashley (1906-1979), author of detective novels under the pseudonym Francis Vivian, requesting a copy of his beekeeping mystery *The Singing Masons*, the sixth Inspector Gordon Knollis investigation, which had been published the previous year in the United Kingdom. The eminent professor wanted the book for Cornell's Everett F. Phillips Beekeeping Collection, "one of the largest and most complete apiculture libraries in the world" (currently in the process of digitization at Cornell's The Hive and the Honeybee website). Sixteen years later Ernest Ashely, or Francis Vivian as I shall henceforward name him, to an American fan requesting an autograph ("Why anyone in the United States, where I am not known," he self-deprecatingly observed, "should want my autograph I cannot imagine, but I am flattered by your request and return your card, duly signed.") declared that fulfilling Professor Phillip's donation request was his "greatest satisfaction as a writer." With ghoulish relish he added, "I believe there was some objection by the Librarian, but the good doctor insisted, and so in it went! It was probably destroyed after Dr. Phillips died. Stung to death."

After investigation I have found no indication that the August 1951 death of Professor Phillips, who was 73 years old at the time, was due to anything other than natural causes. One assumes that what would have been the painfully ironic demise of the American nation's most distinguished apiculturist from bee stings would have merited some mention in his death notices. Yet Francis Vivian's fabulistic claim otherwise provides us with a glimpse of that mordant sense of humor and storytelling relish which glint throughout the eighteen mystery novels Vivian published between 1937 and 1959.

Ten of these mysteries were tales of the ingenious sleuthing exploits of series detective Inspector Gordon Knollis, head of the Burnham C.I.D. in the first novel in the series and a Scotland Yard detective in the rest. (Knollis returns to Burnham in later novels.) The debut Inspector Knollis mystery, *The Death of Mr. Lomas*, which was published in 1941, is actually the seventh Francis Vivian detective novel. However, after the Second World War, when the author belatedly returned to his vocation of mystery writing, all of the remaining detective novels he published, with two exceptions, chronicle the criminal cases of the keen and clever Knollis. These other Inspector Knollis tales are: *Sable Messenger* (1947), *The Threefold Cord* (1947), *The Ninth Enemy* (1948), *The Laughing Dog* (1949), *The Singing Masons* (1950), *The Elusive Bowman* (1951), *The Sleeping Island* (1951), *The Ladies of Locksley* (1953) and *Darkling Death* (1956). (Inspector Knollis also is passingly mentioned in Francis Vivian's final mystery, published in 1959, *Dead Opposite the Church*.) By the late Forties and early Fifties, when Hodder & Stoughton, one of England's most important purveyors of crime and mystery fiction, was publishing the Francis Vivian novels, the Inspector Knollis mysteries had achieved wide popularity in the UK, where "according to the booksellers and librarians," the author's newspaper colleague John Hall later recalled in the *Guardian* (possibly with some exaggeration), "Francis Vivian was neck and neck with Ngaio Marsh in second place after Agatha Christie." (Hardcover sales and penny library rentals must be meant here, as with one exception--a paperback original--Francis Vivian, in great contrast with Crime Queens Marsh and Christie, both mainstays of Penguin Books in the UK, was never published in softcover.)

John Hall asserted that in Francis Vivian's native coal and iron county of Nottinghamshire, where Vivian from the 1940s through the 1960s was an assistant editor and "colour man" (writer of local color stories) on the Nottingham, or Notts, *Free Press*, the detective novelist "through a large stretch of the coalfield is reckoned the best local author after Byron and D. H. Lawrence." Hall added that "People who wouldn't know Alan

Sillitoe from George Eliot will stop Ernest in the street and tell him they solved his last detective story." Somewhat ironically, given this assertion, Vivian in his capacity as a founding member of the Nottingham Writers Club awarded first prize in a 1950 Nottingham writing competition to no other than 22-year-old local aspirant Alan Sillitoe, future "angry young man" author of *Saturday Night and Sunday Morning* (1958) and *The Loneliness of the Long Distance Runner* (1959). In his 1995 autobiography Sillitoe recollected that Vivian, "a crime novelist who earned his living by writing . . . gave [my story] first prize, telling me it was so well written and original that nothing further need be done, and that I should try to get it published." This was "The General's Dilemma," which Sillitoe later expanded into his second novel, *The General* (1960).

While never himself an angry young man (he was, rather, a "ragged-trousered" philosopher), Francis Vivian came from fairly humble origins in life and well knew how to wield both the hammer and the pen. Born on March 23, 1906, Vivian was one of two children of Arthur Ernest Ashley, Sr., a photographer and picture framer in East Retford, Nottinghamshire, and Elizabeth Hallam. His elder brother, Hallam Ashley (1900-1987), moved to Norwich and became a freelance photographer. Today he is known for his photographs, taken from the 1940s through the 1960s, chronicling rural labor in East Anglia (many of which were collected in the 2010 book *Traditional Crafts and Industries in East Anglia: The Photographs of Hallam Ashley*). For his part, Francis Vivian started working at age 15 as a gas meter emptier, then labored for 11 years as a housepainter and decorator before successfully establishing himself in 1932 as a writer of short fiction for newspapers and general magazines. In 1937, he published his first detective novel, *Death at the Salutation*. Three years later, he wed schoolteacher Dorothy Wallwork, with whom he had one daughter.

After the Second World War Francis Vivian's work with the Notts *Free Press* consumed much of his time, yet he was still able for the next half-dozen years to publish annually a detective novel (or two), as well as to give popular lectures on a plethora of intriguing subjects, including, naturally enough, crime, but also fiction writing (he published two guidebooks on that subject), psychic forces (he believed himself to be psychic), black magic, Greek civilization, drama, psychology and beekeeping. The latter occupation he himself took up as a hobby, following in the path of Sherlock Holmes. Vivian's fascination with such esoterica invariably found its way into his detective novels, much to the delight of his loyal readership.

As a detective novelist, John Hall recalled, Francis Vivian "took great pride in the fact that the reader could always arrive at a correct solution from the given data. His Inspector never picked up an undisclosed clue which, it was later revealed, held the solution to the mystery all along." Vivian died on April 2, 1979, at the respectable if not quite venerable age of 73, just like Professor Everett Franklin Phillips. To my knowledge the late mystery writer had not been stung to death by bees.

Curtis Evans

With sincere thanks to all the detectives, policemen, doctors, chemists, editors, journalists, and experts in other fields who have so readily helped me during the past fifteen years.

PROLOGUE

GORDON KNOLLIS has a friend, Brother Ignatius. He is a priest of the Nestorian Order, a little man, lean-bodied and thin-faced, who habitually wears a black skull-cap or a wide-brimmed Franciscan hat, a black cassock, and sandals. From time to time he telephones Knollis at New Scotland Yard to suggest taking lunch at a restaurant round the corner in Bridge Street. On these occasions Brother Ignatius invariably seeks advice or information regarding some problem that has come his way.

Brother Ignatius has a roaming brief. Like his Master, he is on earth to help sinners and the oppressed, and whether you holiday at Brighton in June, or at Perranporth in September, you are quite likely to run into him, looking as much at home as if he was in his quiet little Sussex village of Londsdale St. Peter's.

It was early in the spring of last year when he most recently rang Knollis. He was in town for two days, he said, and would dearly enjoy the opportunity of renewing their friendship—apart from which there was a certain little matter he wished to discuss. If that same day was convenient, and the little place round the corner still in favour . . . ?

The equally lean-faced Knollis smiled to himself as he accepted the invitation. The little priest was one of his favourite friends—not that he saw him more than twice a year at the very most, but the more he saw of him the better he liked him. He was a deceptive little man inasmuch as he covered a penetrating intelligence with a peculiar naïveness of manner. To those who did not know him he appeared most unworldly, an innocent wandering through a not-so-good world and seeing nothing but the beauty of the flowers and the excellent qualities of his fellow-men. When you did know him anything like at all well you soon realised that he could take a problem and reduce it to its essential elements with the ruthless logic to which was added something which Knollis always found difficult to define. If Ignatius had a "certain little matter" which he wished to discuss it would be an interesting luncheon.

They met in the vestibule as Big Ben was chiming the half-hour of twelve o'clock. They shook hands warmly.

"It must be six months since we last met," said Ignatius as he put his thumb-staff in the umbrella stand. He looked Knollis up and down. "You don't alter much, Gordon! Still the same intense features. Still the same sailor's eyes, always half-closed as if searching the horizon. Yes, still as intense as ever! You really should learn to relax! You work too hard, you know!"

"I have to work hard," said Knollis with a smile.

"I'm not referring to the amount of work you have to do, but with the way you go about it," replied Ignatius. "Once you learn to relax, to work relaxed, you can do twice the amount of work in the same time and emerge considerably fresher. You really need some instruction in the newer practical psychology."

He sighed. "However, I must not criticise you, for indeed it is myself who stands in need of criticism today. I feel guilty. I never *seem* to desire your company unless I need your help. That is not the case, of course. There are so many people in the world who seem to need my own help that I have to forgo one of the most obvious pleasures in order to do what I can to ease their lot. But how is the world treating you?"

"I'm bearing up," said Knollis. "Truthfully, things are fairly quiet now. I haven't handled a major case since I went down to Teverby."

"Ah, yes! The bow and arrow case! You brought that off very successfully if you don't mind me saying so. Now—the grill-room?"

Brother Ignatius was a good trencherman, and he liked a drink with his meals, and before meals, and after meals, and indeed at any other time for he did not despise any of the beverages which the good God had placed on earth, or caused men to invent. He did not believe in sin, but only in wisdom and folly. It was not sinful to drink wines, or spirits, or ales, but it was folly if one did not remember how much it was sensible to take, and when to leave off. Like St. Paul, he believed that all things were lawful, but not all things were expedient. So he and Knollis ate, and drank, and talked lightly of the weather, and the burgeoning countryside, and of this, and that, and the other.

With the arrival of coffee Brother Ignatius began pushing the crumbs of biscuit round his plate to form a pattern.

"You will remember the case of Arthur Shardlow?"

Knollis glanced up. "The Sussex policeman who was convicted of breaking and entering some country house?"

"He is now in Parkhurst Prison."

"A good place for him to be," said Knollis. "He got everything he was due to get. We can't have such doings in the police force. One case like that can seriously undermine public confidence in us."

Brother Ignatius glanced up without moving his head. "He was innocent," he said mildly.

"Fiddlesticks!" exclaimed Knollis. "The evidence was overwhelmingly against him. He knew it, too, for he put up no defence."

"The evidence was against him," Brother Ignatius said in a gentle voice. "Er—you will pardon me if I drop into the jargon of the underworld? He was framed."

Knollis out his hands to his head. "Oh, goodness, don't start that, Ignatius! How many times have I heard it! *I was framed, or, I was doped and didn't know what I was a-doing of!* He had a fair trial and the offence was proved beyond any doubt!"

Brother Ignatius sighed. "There had been a spate of country-house robberies, ranging all the way from the outer boundary of the County of London down to the coast. Shardlow had a clue to the identity of the thieves, and was foolish in keeping it to himself. He was ambitious to be transferred to the plain clothes branch, and thought he should produce proof of his initiative before applying for the transfer."

"In which case he was a mug!" Knollis said bluntly. "It makes a good story, anyway!"

"He was becoming dangerous to the safety of the gang", Brother Ignatius went on, not heeding Knollis's comments. "This particular—er—mob did not believe in violence, believing it always resulted in a public outcry which made you people intensify your efforts, and consequently made life more difficult for them. They decided to frame him."

"Okay! Let's have the story since you're determined I shall hear it," said Knollis.

"Shardlow was allowed to come into possession of information to the effect that a certain house would be entered at eleven o'clock on a certain night. It would be empty, the owner and his wife being at some musical comedy show in London. The house was actually entered at nine. The safe was opened, and the contents spread out over the floor of the room. Nothing was taken. Everything was then wiped of—er—dabs. The house was watched. When Shardlow entered by a window which had already been forced, a most harmless-seeming character living in the village telephoned to the police to inform them that one of their own men had been seen breaking into the house. Meanwhile another man made footprints in the borders round the walls of the house with an old pair of Shardlow's shoes which his wife had been persuaded to give to a poor old beggar some days previously—thus tending to prove that Shardlow had reconnoitered the house some time before breaking in. The mobile squad found Shardlow on his knees before the safe, hastily stuffing lady's jewels into a black velvet bag. When asked why he had not telephoned his section house, or divisional headquarters, he pointed to the telephone wires, which were severed."

"There's a point which always interests me," said Knollis. "You mostly drop across it in crime fiction. Telephone wires are always being cut, but it never seems to occur to anyone to bare the severed ends and twist 'em together so that the telephone can be used."

Brother Ignatius nodded into his plate and pushed the crumbs around until they formed a star. "Now his wife has disappeared. They lived in my village, of course. He was our village bobby. I have talked many hours with her since her husband went to prison, and I have read Shardlow's private diary which his wife found hidden in an old desk. The man is undoubtedly innocent!"

"Well?" asked Knollis.

"The case could be re-opened?"

"You'd need overwhelming evidence of the man's innocence in order to get a new trial. Your case would have to be properly prepared and submitted to the Home Secretary. Candidly, Ignatius, by what I remember of the case, you are wasting your time."

"But it could be re-opened if I provided the evidence?"

"You're just asking me to tell you something you already know."

"Thank you very much indeed," Brother Ignatius said politely. "I must really get to work on the case."

They were silent for a while, and then Knollis said, somewhat hesitantly: "You know something of my personal history, don't you?"

Brother Ignatius looked up curiously. "Yes—something."

"I was born in Burnham," Knollis said reflectively with near-closed eyes. "I was educated at the London Road Council School, and the King Edward Grammar School. I entered the engineering profession on leaving school, which was in '26. I pounded the beat for four years, and then, like your friend Shardlow, thought about the C.I.D. I was transferred, sailed through the probationary period, and then promotion set it."

"Yes?"

"During the war I was transferred to the Yard under war-time powers held by the Home Office. There was a shortage of detectives in the metropolis."

He fell silent, and Brother Ignatius again said: "Well?"

"Something happened to me, Ignatius . . ."

"Tell me about it—if you care to do so."

Knollis scratched his head, and gained time to frame his words by offering his cigarettes and lighter.

"Well," he said when two cigarettes were glowing, "until two years ago I thought I had my life and career nicely sewn up—you know, a daily routine planned, and all my methods of working duly organised now and for ever. People were like machines. All you had to do was study 'em, and in time you could say that if a certain character in a case was met by a situation named 'A' he could be relied on to do something named 'B' and something named 'C' was bound to result."

"The law of cause and effect!" said Ignatius. "You expected your fellow men to be machines working on a set and inviolable law."

"You see," Knollis said uncomfortably, "I've always relied on reasoning—well, up to some time ago. It was when I'd come up against a few major murder cases that I began to realise that there was something wrong with me—my—what can I call them? My methods? My philosophy of life?"

"Ah!" exclaimed Brother Ignatius.

"You know what I mean?" asked Knollis.

"You have a department—or a series of files—which you refer to as *Modus Operandi*. In it are filed the peculiarities and idiosyncrasies of habitual criminals. If a robbery is committed, you tabulate the methods which have been used, and then consult your files for the names of those criminals who work in similar ways. Then, in effect, all you have to do is test the alibis of the criminals concerned. Yes?"

"That's correct," said Knollis.

"But murderers are seldom habitual criminals, my dear Gordon. They are usually amateurs, committing their very first crime. A man murdering another for his money, or a woman poisoning a brutal husband, or a good man driven by desperation to the killing of a blackmailer. It is seldom a murderer has previously crossed the boundary between wisdom and folly!"

"Yes, I know that," Knollis said impatiently. "That isn't all of it. Even in a case of that nature I've relied on reasoning—which is surely the logical thing to do. I've gathered all the available facts, and then tried to put them together as if they constituted the parts of a gigantic puzzle—all too often during late years I've come up against a brick wall. My power of reasoning doesn't always give the answers. I've then thrown the whole thing aside and gone to the cinema, for a walk, and *then*—"

"And then," Brother Ignatius interrupted, "much to your surprise the whole solution has jumped into your mind, much as the Greek Athena sprang from the brow of Zeus."

"Yes!" said Knollis. "How did you know?"

"Because that is the way the mind prefers to work, if only you will co-operate by learning to relax, mentally as well as physically. That is what I was trying to tell you out in the vestibule. You are looking older than your age. You are wearing yourself out by doing unnecessary mental work. You see, my dear Gordon, concentration should certainly be practiced during the collection and correlation of the facts. When that is done the rest of the mind, the back room if we may call it that, takes over from your objective mind, and if left to its own devices will provide the answers to your problems."

"But you're suggesting that I should rely on intuition!" Knollis said in a shocked voice.

"Or God," Brother Ignatius said quietly. "See, how long have you been married?"

"I met Jean while on holiday at Shamley Green in '32, and we were married the same year."

"And you have two sons?"

"Edward was born late the following year, and Malcolm was born in '35."

"Dear, dear!" sighed Brother Ignatius. "I hate to think what you must have been like before you were subjected to the mellowing influence of married life!"

"I beg your pardon!" exclaimed Knollis.

"You heard what I said, Gordon! You are a materialist, and a logician gone mad. You have believed that your fellow-men are machines, and you have tried to make yourself into a similar machine—a thinking machine. It won't do, you know! It really won't do! Have you ever read *The Bridge of San Luis Rey*? There is a Brother Juniper in that book who opines that theology should be reduced to an exact science. Now it is obvious that he is guilty of either heresy or a fallacy."

"Couldn't it be reduced?"

Brother Ignatius smiled at him. "If the Universe is a stable machine, governed by laws, then it should be possible to discover those laws, to define them, and understand them, in which case even the Godhead would be capable of analysis and definition. On the other hand if the Universe is a great experiment, or even if it is unfinished, it is still growing, still being created, still in a state of flux—you do see what I mean?"

"No," Knollis said bluntly.

"I have known you for a good many years," said Brother Ignatius. "That is the reason why I can say things to you which would be presumptuous and impertinent in other circumstances. You have been a most self-satisfied man, believing that by asking enough questions and gleaning satisfactory answers you could break down any problem presented to you—all by yourself. When you failed to break a case you blamed it on insufficient evidence, and not on your own lack of perception and reasoning. Then, if your biographer has been completely truthful and has not fallen back on self-made fictions in order to add verisimilitude to otherwise bald and unconvincing narratives, you began to realise there was more in life than you had considered, and more indeed to yourself. Whether you cared to admit it or not, you were tending to rely more and more on intuition. That was abhorrent to you, since you believed—as you still do—that intuition was a purely feminine attribute or faculty. I will not go into deep waters now, but before I leave you I will say that the life of the senses is illusory. It is intuition, an attribute of the soul female, or the soul male, that will always solve your problems for you, and that it is the truth no matter how you attempt to rationalise. Cast aside your embarrassment and learn to rely on it!"

He smiled at Knollis. "See it is my turn to pay for the luncheon, is it not?"

He got up suddenly, leaned across the table, and touched Knollis lightly and almost affectionately on the shoulder.

"Now you have begun to doubt and have started asking questions instead of taking life and yourself for granted, experiences will be put in your way which will help you solve your problems. I know the answers, but you must find them for yourself. There is a very great gulf between intellectual understanding and emotional realisation. And you have not finished with the affairs of Arthur Shardlow".

"Where are you going?" asked Knollis as Brother Ignatius pushed back his chair.

"To try to prevent a murder, Gordon."

Then he was gone, a small black-attired enigma passing through the open doorway and up the stairs to the pay-desk and the street.

Knollis half-rose from the table. He sat down again, knowing it was useless to call after his little friend. Ignatius had put a key in his hands, and he must learn how to use it.

CHAPTER I

BLUEPRINT FOR MURDER

THE VALE OF LOCKSLEY is more like a gulf than a valley, its wooded sides rising steeply from the one road that passes from nowhere in particular to the Borough of Beddington, seven miles to the east, and follows the course of the winding Locksley Stream. It is four miles long, and a mile across as its widest point.

Locksley village is concentrated in a small area halfway through the vale, and comprises of fifty houses and cottages, a school, a chapel of ease, two farms, and an inn run by a man who ekes out his living by working a smallholding, and doing occasional hedging and thatching. Four buses pass through in the course of any one week, all on the same day; two to Beddington market in the morning, and two returning in the late afternoon and early evening. For the rest of the week Locksley is undisturbed except by the delivery vans of Beddington tradesmen, there being no shop of any description in the village.

The social life of the village is concentrated in the school. A whist drive is held there every Wednesday and Saturday night. The youth club meets on Monday evenings at seven o'clock. The Locksley Women's Club congregates every Thursday evening at seven-thirty, and on the second Tuesday of each month the same women meet at the Locksley Vale branch of the Women's Institute. Those with cars, or those who have friends owning cars, go into Beddington to gossip in the smoke-rooms of the

Swan or the New Inn; those without transport either stay at home or take the odd drink at Will Curshaw's Ram & Crook Inn opposite the school.

Mrs. Marion Cartland was the uncrowned squireen of the village, being president of the Women's Institute, and president and patron of the Locksley Vale Youth Fellowship. She was, of course, also chairman of the Women's Club. She was a mature woman of fifty, plump and patronising, and fond of tweed suits that emphasised her full bust and pair of undoubtedly good legs. She had brown hair, and clear-sighted blue eyes which informed her good brain of all that went on in the Vale, and in much of the world outside it. She was possessed of an undeniable flair for organisation, and organised everything in the village, from the renting of the schoolroom to the lying-in arrangements for any woman awaiting her confinement. In an earlier day she would have organised the suffragettes, and made sure that everyone but herself was firmly chained to the railings outside the Houses of Parliament.

Her honorary secretary for both the women's clubs was Mrs. Kathleen Morley, the wife of her husband's business partner, a competent young woman engaged in an undeclared but constant battle with Mrs. Cartland for the reins. She had no chance whatsoever, but being a sticker she hung on like an ambitious understudy, awaiting the day when her principal would fall or break a leg and thus provide the chance she needed to prove her worth.

Mrs. Morley was twenty-eight, and modern. She wore her fair hair shoulder-length, and in an indescribably untidy state which she asserted was all the rage with anybody who was anybody. Like Mrs. Cartland, she favoured suits and costumes, and preferred greys, having read in some book on personal psychology that any shade of grey reveals you as you were, whereas other colours tended to emphasise one's good points and push less desirable ones into the background. She was satisfied that she had nothing to hide. Her face, for instance, was long in the classical tradition, and graced with a long straight nose that compared favorably with that of the plaster Venus de Milo which stood just inside the entrance of the Greek Room in the Public Museum of Burnham, the county capital. Her eyes were a very pale grey, and fringed with long lashes which she knew how to use, particularly on her husband. She had a high waist, a small bust, and long legs which swung from her hips as she walked.

On a fine morning in the middle of June she strode along the vale road to Mrs. Cartland's house, White Gables. By arrangement they were to consider the Women's Institute programme for the coming autumn-winter season. Mrs. Cartland welcomed her effusively, remarked on the sunny weather in the way the English do—as if no one else has noticed it, and led her into the white lounge, to which the part-witted maid brought in coffee and biscuits. They sipped and nibbled, exchanged tidbits of local gossip, lit cork-tipped cigarettes from Mrs. Cartland's ormulu cigarette box, and then settled down to sort out the regular events which always seemed popular with the members—none of whom were of course as educated and intelligent as their president and secretary.

"We'll do the beetle drive?" said Mrs. Cartland. You do think so, Kathleen, dear?"

Kathleen dear was not at all sure. "We could do with a change, *really*," she said daringly. "After all, we've had one every season for five years!"

"We'll include the beetle drive," said Mrs. Cartland, as if she had never heard the objection. "Then the annual whist drive for the Old Age Pensioners' Christmas Parcels. We mustn't forget the Iced Cake and Flower Decoration competitions—and of course we'll need three speakers!"

"Please don't let us have any more basket-makers, bee keepers, or candlewick demonstrators!" pleaded Mrs. Morley. "Nobody in the Vale does candlewick, nobody makes baskets and nobody keeps bees nor wants to keep them!"

"You're correct!" Mrs. Cartland said surprisingly. "We really need something different. I was wondering Kathleen dear . . . There's an author living out at Welsh Meadows. I don't know what he writes, of course, but he *would* be a change if we could get him!"

"Paying him a fee?"

Mrs. Cartland smiled a mirthless smile. "We won't mention that unless he does, dear. He isn't on the panel, so we can assume he doesn't know anything about the usual arrangements. No, unless he says something I shan't mention paying him. After all, if we *can* get him for nothing—well, it all helps the funds! Yes, I think I'll approach him."

"That will be nice!" enthused Mrs. Morley, hugging her knees and dripping cigarette ash down her skirt. "I've always been interested in literature and writing."

"I'll ring him later in the day—I suppose authors *can* be found at home, and awake, during the daytime? I mean, they don't sleep all day and work at night, do they?"

"You're thinking about bats," Mrs. Morley said with a silly giggle.

Mrs. Cartland was staring pensively at the list. "Then again, I was wondering . . . Roger was speaking the other day of the most remarkable man he had met—Sir Edmund Griffin, director of the Home Office Forensic Laboratory at Burnham."

"Oh, yes, please!" said Mrs. Morley, clapping her hands like an adolescent girl. "It would be such a nice change for we people living in this peaceful and crimeless little valley! Like—like a bunch of flowers to a man in prison."

"Your simile is hardly apt, Kathleen dear," murmured Mrs. Cartland dryly. "Anyway, I don't know! I'll think about it before the meeting. Then we'll need a woman speaker to balance the programme. The V.C.O. from Boroughbridge will have to be given a night."

"I'm sick of Visiting County Officers," grumbled Mrs. Morley. "All they tell us is how well other branches are doing—and there isn't a more go-ahead branch in the county than ours!"

"Nevertheless, Kathleen dear, we must invite her. It is expected of us!"

Mrs. Morley stared at her polished nails. "I'll agree if we can have Sir Edmund Griffin as well!"

Mrs. Cartland looked at her as the Queen must have looked at Alice before she cried: "Off with her head!"

"What did you say, dear?" she asked coldly.

"That I'd agree if we could have Sir Edmund," replied Mrs. Morley. She did not look up, and so did not realise the enormity of her offence.

Mrs. Cartland straightened her back. "Kathleen dear, it is not your place to say who we shall and shall not have. *We* draw up a tentative programme for the Committee. If they like it we present it to the branch meeting, and if *they* like it . . ."

Mrs. Morley held her breath for a second. Then she looked up, fluttered her long lashes, and smiled winningly.

"But you know they'll accept anything *you* suggest, Mrs. Cartland."

"They trust my judgement, dear!" Mrs. Cartland replied icily.

"That's just what I mean! They are bound to agree to Sir Edmund if you suggest him."

Mrs. Cartland tried hard to look doubtful. "You—er—think so, dear?"

"I'm sure of it, Mrs. Cartland!"

Mrs. Cartland purred silently for a few moments, and pushed the cigarette box across. Mrs. Morley found her lighter, and held it between the two cigarettes in turn.

"Perhaps you're right, Kathleen dear. Yes, perhaps so! I'll have a word with Roger this evening and see if he can pull any strings. I mean, we can hardly expect Sir Edmund to jump at the opportunity of addressing a group of women of whom he has never heard. And Roger has connections, you know!"

"Yes, I'm aware of it," Mrs. Morley said softly. "He's done everything for Joe and me. We'd never have had money, and we'd never have had Locksley House but for him—and you."

"They make admirable partners, Kathleen. Joe always did admire Roger's business acumen."

Mrs. Morley tightened her lips for a moment. "And Mr. Cartland always admired Joe's craftsmanship!" she retorted.

"Oh yes, dear!" Mrs. Cartland replied. "Roger will admit there isn't a better craftsman outside London! Still—the programme! Now that gives us Sir Edmund, the V.C.O, and the author man from Welsh Meadows. Someone tells me he writes mystery and detective novels. That would be *too* much, would it, do you think?"

"The author won't necessarily talk on crime," Mrs. Morley said quickly. She didn't want to lose either speaker if she could help it. "And even if he does it will still make a nice change from bee-keeping and candlewick! You will ask Sir Edmund to talk on criminals?"

"I suppose so, dear," Mrs. Cartland replied thoughtfully. "Some years ago I read Edgar Allan Poe's essay—no, surely it was de Quincey's!—on the Gentle Art of Murder or some such title. I found myself most interested in the psychology of murder. *The Psychology of Murder!* Perhaps that should be the title, do you think?"

Mrs. Morley tried it over, tasting it with her lips, reading it with the eyes of her mind. "The Psychology of Murder! The Psychology of Murder! Why, it would make the most marvelous title! Think how it will look in the printed programme!

Mrs. Cartland blew twin columns of smoke down her nostrils, and nodded slowly. "That's exactly what I am thinking, dear. Rather an odd title for the programme of a rural woman's society, surely?"

"We do pride ourselves in being modern and progressive," Mrs. Morley said desperately.

"Yes, I think you have me there, Kathleen dear. Very well, we'll leave it in, and hope the members accept it. Sir Edmund Griffin on The Psychology of Murder. Now then; the iced cake, the beetle drive, the flowers, the whist drive, and three speakers take us to the Annual General Meeting. We must keep the ballroom and folk-dancing half-hours in . . ."

That same evening Mrs. Cartland mentioned that matter to her husband, and Roger Cartland got in touch with Superintendent Manson of the County C.I.D., who, had a private word with Sir Edmund Griffin, and as Sir Edmund liked talking, particularly about himself, he asked Manson to tell Roger Cartland that his wife could invite him and he would accept, preferably for the second Tuesday in September, nine days after he was due to retire.

Mrs. Cartland chose to make the night of his visit the annual Guest Night, where husbands of the members were invited, and expected to attend. Sir Edmund, a tall, distinguished-looking man with silver hair and rimless glasses, spoke for an hour and a quarter, proving by the analyses of a dozen well-remembered cases that it was possible and easy to get away with murder providing you planned well, watched your step, and observed a few elementary principles.

At the end, when most of the trivial, and mostly irrelevant, questions had been asked, Mrs. Kathleen Morley rose to address the Chair.

"Madam President," she said, "our speaker has suggested that it is easy to commit a murder in such a way that no suspicions falls on the culprit or any other person at any time. Being a voracious reader of detective novels, I find that statement most intriguing, and wonder if Sir Edmund would be prepared to enlarge on the subject?"

Sir Edmund rose slowly, rubbing his right cheek thoughtfully, and looking askance at Mrs. Morley. "I could have hoped that the particularly question not be asked," he said, "since it is obviously a matter of discussion only in police circles. That being so, I trust I shall not be pressed with supplementary questions when I have said that a murder, to be successful, must never look like such even for one short moment of time. The resulting death must appear to be the result of natural death, accident, or suicide."

He bowed lightly to the Chair, and sat down. There was an embarrassed silence in the room for some seconds, and then Mrs. Cartland hurriedly called on Mrs. Debenham to propose a vote of thanks on behalf of the meeting, and on Mrs. Curshaw to second it. Sir Edmund was then hurried away by Roger Cartland, who beckoned to Joe Morley and two other friends. The five men when to Cartland's house for drinks and a light supper.

"You should never have asked that question," Mrs. Cartland said severely as the door closed behind the men.

"But I was interested!" Mrs. Morley protested. She giggled. "You never know when the information might come in useful!"

"Kathleen!" said Mrs. Cartland.

Chapter II
APPOINTMENT WITH DEATH

BURNHAM IS an incongruous mixture of the new and the old. Openshawe Square, in the centre of the city, bears the name of the freedom-loving burgher who led a group of his fellow-men to the New World when the *Mayflower* sailed from Plymouth Sound, and yet no trace remains there of the age in which he lived; the old market square has been swept away, giving place to a four-acre expanse of stone slabs, bird-baths, and statuary intended to provide a garden of rest and an incidental play-ground for the city pigeons.

Twentieth-Century Burnham is represented by the Square, and by the numerous factories and works and the complementary circle of red-roofed housing estates which surround the city like a shingle-belt. The last traces of the ancient town are to be found in the narrow alleys, courts, and lanes that wind away from the busy commercial centre to where St. Giles' Cathedral dominates the townscape from the two-hundred feet high rock to the north-west of the Square. Here, in the street-names, can be found something of Burnham's historical past—Mayflower Street, Pilgrim Corner, Crusader Lane, Friar's Walk, Fox Street, Quaker Lane, and Spaniel Row.

Spaniel Row is thirty yards long, and only eighteen feet wide. The towering wall of a four-storey lace factory forms the eastern side of it. The western side is shared by an old Quaker burial ground and the Spaniels Inn, which forms the corner of Spaniel Row and Quaker Lane, and is kept by Franklin Wooderson, a slim and dark man of forty.

The inn is over seven hundred years old, a low-ceilinged and heavy-beamed house with deep rock cellars in which past landlords brewed their own ales. It is a popular resort with Burnham-ians, and living proof of the old saying about birds of a feather flocking together. In its long smoke-room can be found the city's professional men; in the large saloon upstairs the boisterous students from the university; in the tap-room the humbler working men, while the be-palmed lounge-bar is the favourite meeting-place of the more heady and colourful younger would-be socialites, a loud-talking set who constitute the lunatic fringe of an otherwise sober and hard-working community.

On Thursday evening, the fourth October of last year, Mr. Wooderson stood in his passage, listening to the last phrases of the regional weather forecasts, and waiting for the six Greenwich pips. When they came they were accompanied by the heavy booming of Old Harry, the bell in the clock-tower of St. Giles'.

Mr. Wooderson drew back the old square bolts and opened the nail-studded oak door, propping it back with an egg-shaped boulder supposed to have been brought home from the Holy Land by some medieval crusader. He went back to his bar, letting the two inner and glass-panelled doors swing to and fro behind him.

Roger Cartland entered the inn at twenty minutes past six. Mr. Wooderson knew him well, and opened a bottle of light ale without waiting for a spoken order. "Nice evening!" he commented.

Cartland merely nodded in reply. He was a heavy-faced man with three chins. His round head was nearly bald, and the wreath of brown hair that remained hung over his collar in an untidy fringe. He was a jeweler, occupying the premises on Pilgrim Corner directly opposite the statue of Daniel Openshawe. Everybody in the city, from Parkinson's Green to Rabbit Hill, knew him, or of him, if only for the remarkable advertisements which appeared every week in the three Burnham papers. No pun was too strained, no slogan too cheap, if he could make his fellow citizens Cartland-conscious, drawing them to his shop to buy their watches and clocks, engagement rings, wedding rings, and birthday and wedding presents.

Watch the Time with Cartland's Clocks! screamed a huge red and black poster pasted to the wall over his doorway.

We'll Ring you if You're Getting Married! Announced a paper banner across his largest window, and indeed Cartland would do that in both senses of the word if your engagement was announced in the *Reporter*, the *Advertiser*, or the *Weekly*

Echo, and if you had the misfortune to be listed in the district telephone directory.

You couldn't get away from Cartland if you lived in Burnham. His name was forced on you from nearly every bill-hoarding in the city, and you soon realised if you were a stranger that here was a man with a flair for publicity who was making money hand over fist. As people always take money to where it is, so Cartland prospered.

If you were a social type you met Cartland all too often in the flesh. He was a member of every worthwhile club and society in the city, and honorary secretary of the Burnham Thursday Society—a luncheon and discussion group. He believed in advertisement, and he believed in contacts. Know everybody worth knowing, and blow your own trumpet as hard as you can, for if you don't nobody else will. The race was to the fastest, and devil take the hindmost.

Cartland emptied his glass and pushed it forward.

"Ditto repeato, and similar," he said flamboyantly. "Have one yourself?"

Mr. Wooderson glanced at the clock. "It's a bit early for me, really. Oh well, thanks," he said as Cartland scowled at him.

"Owe you that for catching you on the hop," said Cartland. "Wife's gone to Wainfleet to see her ailing sister, and I didn't fancy eating alone—especially as the maid we've got is half-witted and quite likely to cook bulbs for onions. I had business to talk over with Joe Morley, so decided to kill two birds with one stone. I rang your wife to see if she could fix a light dinner at short notice."

"No trouble at all," Mr. Wooderson assured him. "That's what we're here for, and we have to be prepared."

"Like the Boy Scouts, eh?" remarked Cartland.

He belched, and did not excuse himself. He unbuttoned his great coat, and then the blue chalk-striped jacket beneath it, and took out a flat package and some crumpled wrapping paper. He handed the wrapping paper to Mr. Wooderson. "Dump that!"

Mr. Wooderson threw it in an empty biscuit tin he kept under the counter for such waste.

When he looked up again Cartland was opening a small flat tin. He flicked back a protecting flap of waxed paper. The box was filled with large white-coated pills. He took one out, flipped it into his mouth, and swallowed it.

"Innards trouble?" Mr. Wooderson asked with the correct amount of sympathy.

Cartland put the box in his waistcoat pocket, and patted his paunch. It replied with a deep baritone rumble.

"Delicate tummy! Wouldn't think it of a man like me, would you? Always have to watch my food—which is why I asked Mrs. W. for fish. These pills are a new formula they've produced. Turned up today with a note asking me to accept them with compliments, and kindly report when I finished them."

He belched again.

"Almost sounds as if they can speak for themselves," said Mr. Wooderson.

"Firm in Leicester," went on Cartland. "Clever little man who runs it. Knows my insides like I know Burnham streets."

"Must be interesting for him!" said Mr. Wooderson.

"Oh, well, they keep going down, so we'll see what happens. Talking of Boy Scouts, did you hear the one about the one who met a girl in the wood who wanted guiding and—"

Mr. Wooderson braced himself for another of Cartland's questionable and usually pointless jokes, but a newcomer opened the swing doors and thankfully cut short Cartland's anecdote.

"Hallo, Joe!" Cartland called loudly. "Fill him a pail of swill, Wooderson!"

"Afraid you'll have to take him home with you for that," said Mr. Wooderson. "I can't compete."

"A glass of bitter, please, Mr. Wooderson," said Mr. Morley with a glance of distaste at Cartland.

Joseph Pevensey Morley was thirty-two, a short and slim-ly-built man with sandy hair, a snub nose, and bright blue eyes. He looked, to Mr. Wooderson, extremely thoughtful if not actually worried.

Until two years ago he owned and occupied the premises on Pilgrim Corner. Cartland bought him out and took over the business. They then formed a partnership and opened up at No.18 Mayflower Street, where Morley practiced as a goldsmith and silversmith, and no longer had to damage his artistic and immortal soul by selling thirty-shilling alarm clocks.

It was a memorable morning in Morley's life when Roger Cartland walked into his shop and planted his podgy forearms on the glass-topped counter.

"Good morning," said Morley.

"You know me? I'm Cartland, from Parkinson's Green. I want to buy your business."

Just like that, blunt and uncompromising.

"I don't want to sell," replied Morley.

"You do," said Cartland, "but you haven't got as far as thinking about it yet. Shall I tell you why? You served your apprenticeship in London, worked as an improver in Birmingham, and came back here. Your father fixed you up in business, hoping to dodge death duties by living the statutory five years. He couldn't make it, and you've been hit damned hard. You're feeling the draught. You're a good craftsman, but a darned rotten businessman. Listen to my offer . . ."

Morley listened, and began to believe in fairies and Santa Claus. Cartland would buy the premises outright. He would buy the stock at trade prices. He would give three thousand for the goodwill. He would buy the shop down Mayflower Street, on which he held an option, and if Morley didn't care to open up there on his own account as a goldsmith and silversmith, then Cartland would go in partnership with him and oversee the business side while Morley attended to the artistic side of the venture.

"You don't really like doing business," added Cartland. "Your heart's in the craft, not in flogging common merchandise to still commoner members of the proletariat. Me, I don't care. I'm only after the money! There's another thing—I'm buying a shop *somewhere* near here, and if I don't buy you out I'll be in competition with you. Think it out. I'll be back."

Morley did think it over. He did so for two days, and then told his wife. Being inherently honest he told her everything

Cartland had said. Kathleen looked round the small suburban home they occupied, and replied, devastatingly: "Mr. Cartland's right, Joe. You're a rotten businessman!"

And that was that. The demoralised Morley found his wife and Cartland pushing him, and on a fine Monday morning he unlocked the new shop and gave his first instructions to the two craftsmen he had employed.

Everything went well from the first. It was just as if he had found Aladdin's ring and lamp and rubbed them. Cartland found them a nice house in the Vale. He arranged for Morley's first-ever car to be delivered immediately despite the fact that his name was the thirty-third on the waiting list. He knew everybody, and soon saw to it that Morley knew everybody, and that everybody knew Morley. He introduced him to the Round Table, the Thursday Society, and the Conservative Club, and with a wink and a nod suggested that other ideas were in the bag.

It all brought business, and Kathleen was suitably impressed by the way the bank balance grew, and no longer played hopscotch between the red and the blue. In less than two years the house was their own, and Morley was gaining an enviable reputation as an artist in precious metals. His *pièce de resistance* was the silver-gilt cruet made for the retiring Lord Mayor to present to the City Plate. That brought an order from the Lord Lieutenant of the County for a rose-bowl trophy to be presented for competition at the University Athletic Meeting, which gave birth to a crop of medals for a horticultural show. So it went, success piling high on success.

Tonight, as Cartland told Mr. Wooderson, they had business to discuss. After another drink they left their coats and Cartland's bowler hat in the cloakroom and went upstairs to the Crusader Room where Mrs. Wooderson was waiting to serve dinner. Morley came down a few minutes later and went to the coin-box at the end of the passage. Mr. Wooderson could not avoid hearing Morley's side of the conversation. He was asking Miss Shawbrook, Cartland's assistant, if they could meet her somewhere in order to borrow her key to the front door of the shop. Mr. Cartland had left his bunch in the office, and needed them later in the evening. She was going to the Theatre Royal and would meet them under the colonnade at eight-twenty, or not later than eight-thirty.

Morley went back upstairs, and almost immediately Cartland came down, muttering something about having left his flipping pills in his coat pocket. He went into the cloakroom, came out a minute later, and went upstairs. An hour later both men came down, both looking extremely serious, both remarkably silent, and Cartland looking, according to Mr. Wooderson, a wee bit pale round the gills.

They each had a whisky, collected their outer garments from the cloaks, and went out without saying goodnight.

That was the last time Mr. Wooderson saw Roger Cartland, dead or alive. At eight-thirty the next morning Superintendent Manson, and Superintendent Lawton of the City C.I.D, called the inn to ask questions about Cartland's visit on the previous evening. It seemed he had met with an accident. Instead of driving straight down the winding hillside to the vale road he had, for some queer reason, turned left and gone along the road that ran along the southern ridge overlooking the vale. He had lost control of the car, and plunged through a gap in the low stone wall. The car had run down the hillside until it came face to face with a sturdy oak tree. The crash was heard by several of the villagers, who raised the alarm and went in search of the crashed car. Cartland was alive when taken from it, but died twenty minutes later.

"A shocking affair!" said Mr. Wooderson.

"He died of poison," said Manson.

"Eh?" exclaimed the startled innkeeper.

"And the Yard are coming down," said Manson. "The Chief Constable would like you to accommodate the bloke who's coming."

Mr. Wooderson tried to add two and two together and make them total more than three "Poison? The Yard? But if he took it himself—"

"Superintendent Manson doesn't think he did," said Lawton.

"Oh!" said Mr. Wooderson. Somehow there didn't seem to be anything else to say. Amidst the confusion of thoughts in his head he dimly realised that the notion of murder was Superintendent Manson's own, and not one necessarily held by anyone else. In some dim way it reminded him of the disclaimer often published in magazines: "The editor does not necessarily associate himself with the opinions of his contributors." But Superintendent Manson thought Cartland had been murdered.

That was actually the case, and Manson had experienced great difficulty in persuading the Chief Constable that Cartland's death was the result of anything but sheer misadventure. It had taken him all night to do so, and he had made the seven-mile journey to Locksley twice before three o'clock in order to provide supporting evidence for his theory.

"Why?" he asked, "should Cartland's car have taken it into its bonnet to run from the road and across the wide grass verge at the only spot on a two-mile length of road where there was a gap in the wall, one caused by an accident a year ago?"

"Coincidence," said the Chief Constable, and gave Manson to understand he was a busy man and a tired man who badly needed sleep. "What does Dr. Robins say?"

"He says," Manson replied heavily, "that Cartland was dying of aconite poisoning, and would be driving subconsciously. The steering would be governed by the camber of the road, and the weight of his arms and hands on the wheel. Instead of going down the winding hillside the camber would lead him gently round the bend—"

"He wasn't the only one who's gone round it," grunted the Chief Constable.

Manson ignored the rudeness of his chief.

"Then Cartland—or the car—drove along until Cartland collapsed over the wheel, swinging the thing over so that he left the road."

"Against the camber," said the Chief Constable, unaware that his remark favoured Manson's case.

"Against the camber, sir," said Manson, nodding his head to emphasise the point. "He and the car, or the car itself, obligingly chose the gap in the wall, passing through with three inches to spare on each side and not even scraping the paint—which means it passed through at right angles to the wall! I don't believe it!"

The Chief Constable snorted. "His gastric trouble got the better of him and he decided to make an end of it."

"Robins says the stomach trouble was not at all serious, sir."

"He won't be the last man on earth to believe his indigestion is cancer of the stomach or something equally stupid!"

Manson closed the door of the office behind him, and swore after it was closed. He went back to his own department and tapped Sergeant Jefferson on the shoulder.

"Get the murder bag, Jeff."

"Going out again, sir?"

"Yes. Ask Grangers to send their breakdown gang and a lorry big enough to take Cartland's car."

Jefferson nodded to one of the detective-officers on duty.

"Grangers in Market Street."

"Let's go," said Manson.

On the ridge road Manson swung the police car at right angles to the gap, and once more inspected the possible clearance. He shook his head. He drove the car through the gap, and braked when the lights were shining on the wreckage of Cartland's car fifty yards lower down the slope.

He and Jefferson walked down to it. It was still in a mess inside, for Cartland had been very ill indeed. Apart from that there was no clue that would have satisfied the reader of a crime novel—no cigarette ash, no spent matches, and nothing in the glove box, the home of good clues, but an A.A. Handbook, a set of folding maps, a dirty plug, and a new unwrapped one. The petrol gauge registered nought, being broken. The mileometer registered 19, 432 miles. The tyres were in good condition. The windscreen was broken. The front wings and the bonnet looked like the remains of a decrepit concertina.

"You don't believe it, do you?" asked Jefferson.

Manson gave a wry smile. "I knew Roger Cartland pretty well, Jeff, and if ever a man cherished life that man did! He was lousy with money, had a good wife, a nice home, and all the glory of his own imagination and the unimaginative citizens of Burnham could shower on him. No, it stinks!"

He looked at the car for a moment.

"Take off the steering wheel, Jeff. Handle it as you'd handle the woman you love."

He corrected himself. "No, handle it like eggs."

When the breakdown gang arrived he gave his instructions. "Keep your hands off all polished surfaces. Don't open the doors. Park the thing in the middle of the courtyard behind my office so's we can get all around it without any trouble. We'll get back now."

Once more in his office he sent the wheel to the fingerprints department, and went to look at the tray on which were laid out the contents of Cartland's pockets. There was a gold cigarette case, and a lighter to match; a handful of small change, a penknife, a latch-lock key, the flat tin of pills from his waistcoat pocket, a cheque-book, a gold-nibbed fountain pen, and a wallet containing five one-pound notes and two ten-shilling notes. And nothing else.

Manson picked up the box to read the label. It informed him that the contents were made up from Formula 121a, and were made by Grove and Meadow of Leicester. There was another label on the bottom of the tin, and this stated the formula. The pills contained dandelion, skullcap, mandrake, golden seal, valerian, and a variety of other herbs mostly unknown to him. He turned the tin the right way up again and noted that while the label was printed the "a" in "121a" had been written in with pen and ink.

He put it back on the tray and stooged round the office until a knock sounded on the door A little man entered. He was known as Dabs although formally christened Samuel Johnson.

"The steering wheel, sir?"

"Well?" asked the tired Manson.

"Completely clean except for three patches—one at ten o'clock, and the others at two o'clock. Palm prints, sir."

A slow smile spread over Manson's round face.

"Lead on, MacDabs!" he said.

Jefferson joined them as they walked through the outer office. In the fingerpints department they stared happily at the white-dusted steering wheel.

"Two palms, *and* the ball of one thumb, Jeff! So he drove through the city streets, and all the way to Locksley like that, did he? And wiped the wheel clean before he started out! It was accident, was it? It was coincidence that he drove through that gap without scraping the sides, and that the car left the road at right angles? Nuts!"

He turned to Johnson. "Get photos as soon as you can."

"Getting the C.C.?" asked Jefferson.

"You know the answer!"

"In ten seconds the time will be exactly three o'clock," said Jefferson.

"Then get the old buzzard out of bed for me," said Manson. "I fail to see why we should be the only bods to lose our beauty sleep. You know, Jeff, this is going to be a job for the Yard."

CHAPTER III
BABBLINGS OF IDIOCY

KATHLEEN MORLEY was turning away from the telephone when she saw the watery forms of two men through the panel of hammered glass in the front door. The bell rang, and she opened the door.

She knew Superintendent Manson, and she knew he had called to ask questions about Roger Cartland. So had the second man, but she did not know him. He was wearing a grey overcoat and a grey velour trilby, a lean man, clean-shaven, with narrow eyes, as carven and impersonal as the bronze bust of St. Giles in the cathedral at Burnham; a remote man who seemed to be trying to look straight through to her thoughts. The smile he granted her was mere polite creasing of the lips, and was certainly not reflected in his eyes—where all genuine smiles should begin. She decided she wasn't going to like him.

She was trying to think who he could be, and then, somehow, both men were in the hall, and door was closed behind them, and Superintendent Manson was saying something to her. She shook herself, forced her attention from the second man, and said: "Yes?"

"We've been to see your husband at his shop in Mayflower Street," Manson repeated.

She nodded. Joe had just rung to tell her about that. He said they'd grilled him as if they thought he was responsible for Roger's suicide or whatever it was supposed to be. There was something very wrong somewhere, and she was to watch her step if they called on her.

"You know that?" said Manson.

"I've just finished talking to my husband," she said indicating the telephone behind the door.

"Before we go any further," said Manson, "please allow me to present Inspector Knollis, of New Scotland Yard."

Kathleen forced a smile of greeting to the somber-faced detective. So this was the man who claimed so much space in the newspapers—almost as much space in the dailies as Roger had claimed in the locals. Roger had paid for his fame, if that word could be used, while this—this sphinx of a man had earned it both by his mental capabilities and his reputation for being unsociable with the gentlemen of the Press.

"How do you do, Inspector," she said flatly.

"Sorry to disturb you like this," he said softly, and she knew he did not mean a word of it.

She stared at him, suddenly realising that it was only twelve hours since Roger died, and yet this Knollis of the Yard was already in Locksley Vale. The time was not yet ten o'clock. It meant—it could only mean . . .

"At what time did your husband arrive home last night?" Manson was saying.

"His car was in dock, and Roger—Mr. Cartland—had promised to pick him up and run him home. I was told the news about Mr. Cartland about twenty to ten, and so of course I rang Joe to tell him. He said he would catch the last bus home. That meant he had to walk from the lane-end, because the bus doesn't run through the Vale."

"You knew Mr. Cartland pretty well?" asked Manson.

"Well, yes, I suppose we did."

"Can you suggest any reason why he should have taken his life?"

Kathleen blinked with surprise. "But there are rumours that he was—was *murdered*."

"Who says that?" Manson asked quickly.

"Well, *they* say so—you know—common gossip," Kathleen replied, and tried to conceal her confusion.

"Do you think he was murdered?" interrupted Knollis.

Kathleen gave an uncertain laugh. "Well, Inspector, I wasn't sure until a few minutes ago, and now I think he was murdered."

"Why so?"

She was regaining her nerve now, and was almost perky as she asked: "Do the Yard come down to the provinces to investigate suicide cases, Inspector?"

Knollis shrugged. "Not as a general rule, Mrs. Morley, but it has been known to happen. I take it you read detective fiction?"

"Oh, yes, and all the books that are written by retiring chief-inspectors and superintendents. So little happens in this vale that a spot of vicarious adventure is necessary to save us from ennui and monotony."

"Then you'd probably enjoy the talk that Sir Edmund Griffin gave at your Women's Institute meeting?" said Manson.

"It was a pretty good talk," Kathleen said softly.

"You are an intelligent woman, Mrs. Morley," said Knollis.

"Thank you, Inspector," she said with a mock bow.

"Can you give us a short résumé of the talk?"

"I can do better! I can show you a transcription of it. I took it down *verbatim* and typed it out the next morning."

"Why on earth . . . ?" Manson murmured.

"You do shorthand, obviously," said Knollis.

"I was a secretary before I married."

"And you have a typewriter."

"Yes, of course," she replied. She hesitated for a second, and then added: "I don't say anything about it in the Vale, but I'm trying to learn to write short stories—crime stories with a romantic background."

"Which explains everything," said Knollis with an unexpected smile which immediately charmed her and disarmed her at the same time. "You have a copy of Sir Edmund's talk. I wonder if I could have the loan of it?"

"If I can have it back!"

"I'll have a copy typed, and send your own straight back. It was a good talk, Mrs. Morley—from your angle as a crime writer?"

"Ye-es, too good for a group of laymen, I think. From my point of view it was super. He analysed a dozen or so murder cases and showed us that it was possible to get away with it providing we use our brains. I got at least half a dozen possible stories from it."

"How helpful!" murmured Knollis. "How many people were present that evening?"

"Probably sixty or seventy. You see, we have thirty-five members, and Mrs. Cartland made it our annual guest night when husbands and friends come along."

"Somewhat increases the odds," said Manson dryly.

"Your husband and Mr. Cartland were present?" asked Knollis.

"Yes, Inspector. Afterwards they went up to Cartland's house for a drink—taking Sir Edmund, of course."

She glanced cautiously at Knollis and ventured a question. "Are these questions about Sir Edmund's talk significant?"

Knollis smiled at her. "Everything's significant, and nothing's significant in a murder investigation. At the moment we're merely doing what the politicians call exploring every avenue."

"And—and he really was murdered?"

"He died of aconite poisoning, Mrs. Morley, and would have done so whether he had crashed the car or not."

"Aconite," said Kathleen wonderingly.

"Obtained from the root of the monkshood plant," explained Knollis. "The plant is also called wolfsbane, and country people call it grandmother's bonnets. It grows about three feet high, and has purple-blue bell-shaped flowers with a hood over them—a monk's hood, you see. The root is similar in shape to horse-radish, and both deliberately and in error it has been used to make horse-radish sauce."

"We've none in our garden!" Kathleen said quickly.

Knollis smiled again. "I was going to ask that, because it would seem obvious that the person who obtained it for the purpose of poisoning Mr. Cartland would not take it from his or her own garden."

"Would you care to look round, Superintendent?"

Manson shook his head.

"What do you know about Roger Cartland?" asked Knollis. "You see, Mrs. Morley, I come to this district as a stranger, knowing nobody connected with the case."

"But surely you were born in Burnham, Inspector? Didn't you serve with the C.I.D. there?"

"That," Knollis said gently, "was ten years ago. Shall we say I am virtually a stranger to the district? Now, what do you know about the Cartlands?"

"Well," said Kathleen, and related the whole of the Morley connections with Roger Cartland and his wife.

"So you didn't know Cartland until he walked into your husband's shop and suggested buying the business?"

"That's correct, Inspector—except that we knew him by repute. Even when he was down at Parkinson's Green he publicised himself pretty well, and we used to laugh over his advertisements."

"Superintendent Manson's told me about them," said Knollis, smiling dryly. "He seems to have been quite good at drawing attention to himself."

"It brought business—to all of us," Kathleen said reflectively. "But for Roger we'd still be struggling to make a very poor living. He was the cleverest businessman I've ever known."

"You and your husband are grateful to him?"

"Oh-my-goodness-yes," she replied in one breath.

"As you've read a good deal of detective fiction, you'll know we have to ask one very stupid question," said Knollis. "Had Roger Cartland any enemies?"

"Roger! He was tremendously well-liked!"

"No odd person to whom he did an ill-turn? No person he—ha-hum—*shopped*?"

Kathleen paused, one finger tentatively tracing the bow of her upper lip. The word *shopped* had rung a bell in her mind. There was someone who had been shopped by Roger!

"You mean Gentleman Davidson?" she said as the name popped into her consciousness.

Manson raised an eyebrow. "That's right, Knollis! Davidson! He went—"

Knollis restrained him by laying a hand on his sleeve. "Let Mrs. Morley tell me, please. What did Gentleman Davidson do, Mrs. Morley?"

"He tried to sell the Salisbury jewels to Roger. It was last autumn, and Davidson went into Pilgrim Corner and offered—let me think! Yes, there was a lady's gold wristlet watch, a bangle, a pearl choker, and matching earclips. He said he had fallen on hard times, that his wife was desperately ill, and that he simply had to sell them, heirlooms though they might be. He'd tried pawning them, and couldn't raise enough on them, so they'd have to go for good."

"And then?"

"Roger recognized them as the stuff stolen from Lady Diana Salisbury's flat at Redhill in Surrey. He stalled Davidson by saying he would need time to value them, and he was just going to his Thursday Society luncheon. He asked him to return just before closing time, and gave him a ten-shilling note on account in case he wanted to buy a meal. When Davidson had gone he phoned the police."

Knollis turned to Manson. "What happened next?"

"I went down, taking a sergeant with me. We didn't know who Davidson was then, because he hadn't left his name. We checked the stuff, and satisfied ourselves that Cartland was correct. We went back later, taking the way down to St. Giles' Lane to the rear of the premises. Davidson didn't turn up, so I phoned H.Q. and put out a general alarm. He was picked up at Victoria, just boarding the London train. He was sent down to Guildford, of course—"

"Guildford?" exclaimed Knollis. For some reason he was unable to explain the name *Shardlow* leapt into his mind. "Go on," he said brusquely.

"We couldn't prove anything but possession, so he only go the usual."

"Which means he'll be out by now!"

"So far as I could make out," said Manson, "he got fed up with the prices his fence was paying him, and decided to try private disposal. He was just plain unlucky in dropping across a man like Cartland who very obviously studied the lists of stolen property we circulated. It was a luck stroke for Cartland, too, bringing him quite a spate of publicity."

Kathleen Morley nodded. "Roger said the case was worth at least three hundred thousand pounds to him, and jokingly suggested giving Davidson commission on sales when he came out."

"That wasn't funny," snorted Knollis. "Anyway, Manson, you'd better find out where Davidson is—just in case."

He turned to Kathleen Morley. "This is some useful information you've given us. You've really something to write about now, haven't you?"

"I'm—I'm not sure I'll want to write about it, Inspector," she replied uncertainly. "Murder isn't quite the same thing when it comes to your own door."

"You've discovered that, have you? Oh well, we'll get along and see if Mrs. Cartland is home from Wainfleet. Thanks for everything, Mrs. Morley."

Knollis and Manson went along the Vale road to the magnificent Cartland house, White Gables. It stood high on a bank, a double-fronted house with an extensive garden descending steeply to the roadway in three terraces. On the gable high above the front door sat a terracotta imp, facing the world with its fingers to its nose.

Manson pointed to it. "Cartland, in effigy, cocking a snook at his fellow-men. That was his private attitude. Despise 'em, and use 'em."

He glanced up the drive that ran along the left of the grounds. There was a branch that turned right towards the front door. The main drive went straight on to a double garage, the sliding doors of which were open.

"Not home yet, Knollis. No car in."

"We'll walk round the garden. We might find the monks-hood."

A vacant-eyed, loose-jawed girl of about seventeen years of age appeared at the doorway and gaped at them.

"Wan' somebody, sir?"

"Is Mrs. Cartland at home?" asked Knollis.

"Gone Burnham t'see p'licemen."

"That's useful, anyway," said Knollis. He lowered his voice to a whisper. "Might be worth while to have a word with the girl. She may know something."

"I doubt if she knows anything," Manson replied caustically.

They walked across the lawn on the second terrace, and up the steps which led through a wide rockery to a red-gravelled path and the front door.

"You'll be Mrs. Cartland's maid?"

"Come in ev'ry morning."

"Did Mr. Cartland take tea at home yesterday?"

"Must 'ave," she said with a senseless giggle.

"Why?"

"Pots washed up and put away."

"You left his tea ready for him?"

She nodded.

"What's your name, miss?" asked Knollis.

"Gabby."

"Short for Gabrielle?"

"Gabrielle Jones."

Manson snorted. "A most interesting and enlightening con-versation, I must say!"

"Shurrup," said Knollis.

"Oh, well," sighed Manson.

"Did you know Mr. Cartland was coming home for tea, Gabby?"

"No. Leffit in case he come. He et it and washed up for me."

"What did you leave for his tea, Gabby?"

"Brenbutter, tea ready in pot, beef in pantry."

"Beef!" said Knollis. "What did Mr. Cartland eat with his beef? He asked purringly. "Sauce? Pickles?"

"You're tempting coincidence," muttered Manson. "I shan't believe it even if she tells you!"

"Hoss-radich," said Gabby.

Manson groaned. "Death by misadventure! And we've fetched you from London. Why didn't I think of it!"

Knollis was as smooth as silk on his beat behaviour at the Old Bailey. "I don't suppose you've any of that sauce left, have you?"

"Swilled away," she said briefly, and stood twisting her gingham apron round her bony hands.

"Who made the sauce, Gabby?"

"Gabby."

"Where did you get the horse-radishes from?"

"Sand."

"She's nuts," said Manson.

"They store 'hoss-radich' in sand-heaps, my dear man," said Knollis placidly. "Care to show me the sand, Gabby?"

She wiped her nose on her gingham apron, and again on her bare arm, and led the way round the side of the house to a sand-heap behind a large greenhouse. She delved with her hands and produced half a dozen horse-radishes.

"These are the real thing, anyway," said Knollis. "Wolfbane is brownish. Listen, Gabby. You got them yourself from this heap, and took them in the kitchen and made the sauce yourself?"

"Gabby do ever'thing round 'ere," she said.

"I can believe that," grunted Manson.

Knollis thoughtfully fingered his chin, and glanced at the part-witted girl, who was again trying to tie her apron into knots. "Like flowers?" he asked.

"Flowers pretty," she said eagerly.

"You know their names?"

"Flowers Gabby's friends. Flowers an' stars."

"Got any grandmother's bonnets in the garden?"

"At 'ome. None in Mis' Cartland's garden."

Knollis looked round and found a rake. With it he demolished the heap of sand. He examined every horse-radish he found, and then carefully raked the heap together again.

"Oh, well!" he signed, and strolled slowly back towards the front door.

"Who takes in the mail, Gabby?" he asked the girl as she jog-trotted along by his side. "You know—letters and parcels."

"Gabby does?"

"How often does he call?"

"B'eakfas' and af' lunch."

"See," said Knollis thoughtfully, "didn't Mr. Cartland have a small parcel yesterday?"

For the first time the light of intelligence glowed in her watery eyes. "Packet for Mis' Cartland," she chanted. "Packet for Mis' Car'land. Postie brought it. Postie brought packet for Mis' Car'land. Mis' Car'lan's packet bought by postie."

"For God's sake turn her off!" Manson said in a low voice. "She'll drive me mental myself!"

Knollis deliberately walked across his toes.

"So Mr. Cartland would find it when he came for his tea, eh, Gabby."

"Gabby put it on Mis' Car'land's plate. Postie bought packet for Mis' Car'land."

Manson put a hand to his head. "Oh, Lord! She's off again!"

"You lock up the house when you go home?" asked Knollis.

"Pull back door. Gabby pulls back door an' it locks."

"Latch lock," Manson said unnecessarily.

Knollis nodded. "Better get back now. We might meet Mrs. Cartland returning if she hasn't found us at H.Q. You know her car?"

"I know it's an Oberon Fourteen—grey one."

"That's near enough," said Knollis.

He gave Gabby a half-crown. She smiled foolishly as it lay in her palm. "Postie brought packet for Mis' Car'land. Postie brought packet for Mis' Car'land—"

Manson strode off down the drive. "That record will send me crackers, Knollis!"

"You might be like it yourself some day," said Knollis as he fell in step with him. "When you reach the sere and yellow leaf you might be talking worse than that—and the odds are that you won't be a quarter as useful. Patience, Manson! *Gently scan they brother man; still gentler sister woman*," he quoted.

They did not meet Mrs. Cartland, but found her waiting patiently for them at headquarters.

"I'm very sorry," said Manson, removing his hat.

"Thank you, Mr. Manson," she replied with dignity. She took a deep steadying breath. "I've done my weeping for the time being. I came straight here after calling at the house. What can I do? Is there anything I can do?"

"First let me introduce Inspector Knollis. He's from the Yard."

"So it was—murder," she said softly.

"We think so, ma'am. We can't see anything else for it—can you?"

"Roger wasn't a coward, and he would not have put an end to his own life, Mr. Manson. He had no reason to do so, either. He had no troubles whatsoever. Our married life was happy, and his business successful."

"No enemies?"

She grimaced. "Enemies, no. People who were envious of him, perhaps. He was a successful self-made man, likely to be envied."

"He and his partner . . ." asked Knollis.

"The best of friends! Roger and Joe respected each other's qualities. It may not sound well coming from me, but Roger was solely responsible for the Morley's sudden rise in the world. They had to thank him for everything."

"Has Mr. Cartland any staff at the shop?"

"Miss Shawbrook only. She's his counter-assistant, secretary, and general manageress all rolled into one."

"How long has she been with him?"

"About six months. She came with the highest references. Why do you ask, Inspector?"

"Merely trying to sketch in the background," said Knollis. "Where does she live?"

"She has a flat in Cavendish Buildings, off Museum Street."

"You see," said Knollis, "she may have seen some trivial incident in the shop about which you know nothing. It's the trivialities which count in these cases, and husbands don't always find it necessary to tell their wives everything that happens in the shop."

"Roger certainly didn't," Mrs. Cartland said ruefully. "I'm calling on Miss Shawbrook when I leave here. I want to persuade her to come out to Locksley for a fortnight and put me *au fait* with the business arrangements. I hope she'll agree, otherwise I may have to sell the business. That's how much I know about the shop on Pilgrim Corner!"

"You will know all about the Davidson affair, of course?"

"Oh, yes! Roger was rather proud of himself over that. He always read the circulars you sent round, and he said it was just the fact that Davidson put them all before him together that caused him to be suspicious. He'd been reading about them that very morning! He said he took the risk of being made to look a fool by the police, but he never refused to take a risk, and like all his other risks and gambles it came off. The publicity was worth pounds to him—and of course a dangerous criminal was given his deserts."

"We could almost regard him as an enemy," said Manson slowly, and glanced at Mrs. Cartland to see how she reacted to the suggestion.

"Why, ye-es! Of course!" she replied. "I never thought of that!"

"How bad was his tummy, Mrs. Cartland?" asked Knollis, anxious to steer Manson from the Davidson angle.

She smiled wryly. "Not very bad, Inspector. Like most of you men he relished a little pampering and fussing, and if it hadn't been his tummy it would have been something else. He liked the attention paid to him by the herbalists, and they liked the cheques he paid them, so everybody was happy. I let him have his little spot of bother, and ignored the fact that he ate like a horse, and could eat almost anything."

"What didn't he like, Mrs. Cartland?"

"Shellfish, tomatoes, and tartare sauce. Queer, isn't it?"

"It's very queer," said Knollis, "especially as he and Mr. Morley partook of plaice and tartare sauce at the Spaniels!"

CHAPTER IV
ALADDIN'S CAVE

WHEN MRS. CARTLAND had gone Knollis looked at the tray of belongings taken from Roger Cartland's pockets. He took up the tin box of pills and examined the label thoroughly.

"He took these things regularly?"

"Not these particular ones," said Manson. "According to Wooderson they were a new sample received by Cartland that day. Cartland explained 'em as a new formula they were trying out on him. Big 'uns, aren't they?"

"Four grains," said Knollis.

They both looked round as the door opened and Sir Edmund Griffin walked in.

"Hello, Manson! Why, Knollis as well! So they've brought you down to solve Burnham's latest mystery, have they? How are you? It must be every bit of five years since we last met."

Sir Edmund hitched his grey trousers, and perched his long body on the edge of Manson's desk. "So we have Gordon Knollis back in Burnham, eh? Well, well! This is most interesting!"

Knollis nodded solemnly. "There's one little matter on which I'd like first-hand information, Sir Edmund—the talk you gave to the women in Locksley Vale."

"I thought that would come up," said Sir Edmund calmly. "Anyone care for a cigarette? No? You won't mind if I smoke in your office, Manson? Thanks."

He took his time over lighting up, and looked whimsically over his rimless glasses. "I understood I was not in the good books over that, Knollis. Lawton told me it had not been favourably received in official quarters. And yet I didn't tell them anything vital, you know!"

"Only the easier ways of bumping off a fellow citizen," Manson commented bitterly.

"Nothing of the kind, Manson! It was a very elementary and academic address."

"It can hardly have been both," remarked Knollis.

Sir Edmund waved a vague hand. "Well, you know what I mean! It sounded awfully authoritative and yet was completely elementary."

"I think we'd better skip the definition," said Knollis. "We aren't doing too well with it. It may be considered impertinent considering how much of my trade I learned by sitting at your lectures, but the fact remains that the Locksley talk was far too hot for a lay audience!"

Sir Edmund stared mildly through his glasses. "You aren't suggesting that my talk was the cause of the Cartland murder, surely?"

"I'm suggesting it might have triggered off the affair," Knollis said bluntly. "You pointed out the mistakes made by a dozen murderers, and wind up by telling a questioner that a good murder should like accident, suicide, or natural causes!"

"You're remarkably well-informed," said Sir Edmund.

"A lady present took a *verbatim* report."

Sir Edmund nodded sagely. "Think she needed the information for a specific purpose?

"Yes," replied Knollis. "She's interested in writing crime fiction."

"Oh, well," said Sir Edmund, "when do I stand in the church porch clothed in a white sheet? What can I do to atone?"

Knollis ignored his mocking, sarcastic tone. He opened the box of pills and tipped six of them into Sir Edmund's hand. "Analyse those for me, please. You still have facilities at the laboratory?"

"I don't need them, Knollis. I have a private lab at my home. You shall have a report in twelve hours."

"Six," said Knollis.

"Six," agreed Sir Edmund. "You think they might have been—"

"I don't know," said Knollis. "I've had but a few hours on the case, but Dr. Robins tells Manson—"

"What does Dr. Robbins tell Manson?" asked a voice from the doorway, and the tubby, red-cheeked police surgeon joined them.

"It's this way," said Knollis. "I've asked Sir Edmund to analyse the pills. You see, Cartland ate lunch at the Thursday Society meeting. He had tea at home—cold beef and horse-radish sauce. He had plaice and tartare sauce at the Spaniels. Either of the sauces could have been used as a cover for the aconite. On the other hand, the pills could have been responsible for Cartland's death."

"They have come from a reputable firm," said Manson, shaking his head as if dissatisfied with Knollis's lack of perception.

"Substitution has been known," said Knollis.

"You can rule out the Spaniels' meal," said the doctor. "He had that meal at seven o'clock, and he died at nine-thirty. You know your physiology as well as I do, and I don't need to tell you how long it takes for grub to get down into the small intestines."

"So what?" asked Manson.

"Most of the aconite was in his bowel, having passed through his tummy. That rules out the Spaniels' meal. On the face of the evidence, the aconite was either in his teatime meal, or in those pills—and to be perfectly honest I'm not satisfied that it was in his tea!"

Griffin eased himself from the table. "I'll slip home and analyse those pills. It seems to me you can do little until you have a report on them. You'll then have something to work on, or can eliminate them completely and look in other directions."

"And I'll get back to the Spaniels for an early lunch, and be ready for a long afternoon," said Knollis. "See you later, Manson!"

He walked down the long corridors to the street with Sir Edmund, who still wore a smile on his aristocratic features.

"Get in," he said. "I'll run you there. It isn't out of my way."

Knollis murmured his thanks, and got in the car.

"Still cross with me?" Sir Edmund enquired as he turned the ignition key and pressed the starter.

"No, Sir Edmund. I'm merely puzzled with the case. Know much about Cartland?"

"A first-rate exhibitionist, of course," said Sir Edmund, lowering his head and squinting sideways over his glasses. "A man of whom I could be most suspicious!"

"Why?" asked Knollis with rising curiosity. He knew Sir Edmund as a man of good intellect, and respected his opinions.

"Can you spare half an hour?"

"I can. Yes."

"Then we'll pull in at the Ambassador, and you shall lunch with me."

Sir Edmund drove under the arch and into the car-park of the city's most select hotel. He led Knollis into the White Hall, and found a table in a discreet alcove.

"Time is valuable to you," he said, "so we'll dismiss the conventions and talk murder over the soup. Now we need a drink . . ."

When the meal was ordered Knollis asked: "Why could you be suspicious of Cartland, Sir Edmund?"

"Hm? Well, for one thing he was living at a pace inconsistent with his income. You see, Knollis, he paid Morley a really astounding figure for the business at Pilgrim Corner, and he bought the Mayflower Street premises as well. He has a marvellous house in Locksley . . ."

"I saw it this morning," said Knollis.

"He ran two cars—shared by his wife, of course. He was a member of nearly every worthwhile club and society in town, and those things cost money, you know! Now the main point is this; if he had been at Pilgrim Corner before he lashed out so lavishly I could have understood it, because the man certainly made money there. But before he went to Pilgrim Corner he was just a suburban jeweler, selling trinkets, mending watches, and so on."

"Yes?" murmured Knollis, having no intention of breaking Sir Edmund's train of thought.

"Know anything of a man named Davidson?"

Knollis waited until the soup was served before replying. "I heard about him this morning—first from Mrs. Morley, and then from Manson. I heard the whole story from two sides."

Sir Edmund nodded gravely over his plate. "There was a peculiar circumstance about that affair, Knollis, and I believe I was the only person to notice it. The stuff Davidson offered to Cartland had been missing for a mere few hours, comparatively speaking. Why Davidson chose to travel down from London to Burnham, *and* pick on Cartland is a matter of conjecture, but the fact remains that Cartland *recognised the stuff as soon as he saw it*! Cartland—a provincial jeweler. Now Davidson virtually admitted trying to sell the stolen property privately because he had not been getting enough from his regular fence."

"Yes," said Knollis thoughtfully.

The waiter removed the soup plates, and returned with the fish.

"You know the game as well as I do, and perhaps better," went on Sir Edmund. "The fence these days is the master mind—and the crime writers are correct in that assumption! He chooses the venue, plans the affair, chooses the men to do the job. In effect he doesn't buy the stuff from the cracksman, but pays him for doing the job! Right?"

"Right!" said Knollis.

"So that, again in effect, Davidson decided to leave the organisation to which he was attached, and branch out on his own account?"

"Ye-es, that's quite a point, Sir Edmund!"

"Now in Parkhurst Prison is a man—"

Knollis looked up, and blinked. "Shardlow! The Sussex policeman!"

"You've heard of him."

"This is queer," remarked Knollis. "I was asked only a few months ago if the case could be re-opened, if a new trial could be arranged."

"That would be Brother Ignatius!"

Knollis stared. "You know Brother Ignatius?"

"Ignatius and I are very old friends. He is in the neighbourhood of Burnham now, believing that certain clues have led him to the centre of the mystery surrounding Shardlow's conviction."

"This—this is getting fantastic!" exclaimed Knollis. "It means—it can only mean that Cartland was—"

Sir Edmund smiled slyly. "Shall we say he was somehow mixed in a very shady business?"

"You were leading to this right from the beginning?"

"Just so," said Sir Edmund.

Knollis narrowed his eyes and stared across the table.

"How do you come to be so interested in this particular case, if I may ask the question?"

Sir Edmund shrugged his shoulders and spread his hands. "I'm no more interested in this case than in any other—and certainly no less Like yourself, my life has been dedicated to the investigation and suppression of crime. Apart from which, also like yourself, I'm interested in any intellectual problem."

"You would be more interested with Cartland being a Burnham man."

"Plus the fact that I lived in Sussex for some years and knew some of the members of Shardlow's family. I'm satisfied on several points, Knollis. First, with due regard to what Cartland was earning while at Parkinson's Green he spent more than he possessed. Secondly, that his act of buying out Morley and installing him in Mayflower Street amounted to an act of charity—and Cartland was not a man addicted to charitable actions. Thirdly, he recognised the Salisbury jewels all too readily. Fourthly, he was the last man in town likely to commit suicide. And fifthly, all my intuitions tell me he was a shady character masquerading as an upright man!"

"Intuitions!" said Knollis. "You believe in 'em?"

"Nobody but a fool can afford to ignore them," replied Sir Edmund. "Now, shall we pay due attention to this most excellent food? How long have you known Ignatius?"

"Does anybody know him?" Knollis countered with a wry smile. "I've been acquainted with him for many years but I know little enough about him. What do you know of him?"

Sir Edmund grimaced. "Very little, really. I know he was ordained by a Nestorian bishop who is resident in London. I know he has a queer kind of wandering brief. I know you will find him wherever someone is in deep waters. I know him as a most discreet man, a man of remarkable intellect, and—yes, a complete enigma. He would help you to prove a man innocent, but would not raise a hand to help you apprehend a guilty one—even, say, the murderer of Roger Cartland. Yes, if Ignatius has interested himself in this case you may look for some amazing twists and turns in it. You are limited by Judges' Rules. Ignatius is limited only by the dictates of his conscience."

Knollis went to the Spaniels Inn after lunch, and had a long interview with Mr. Wooderson, encouraging him to remember every possible detail of Cartland's visit on the previous evening.

"You still have the wrapping paper he gave you?" he asked.

Mr. Wooderson thought he could find it, and went through to the bar, returning with it a minute or so later.

"It probably means, nothing," said Knollis, "but it does carry the address of the firm in case we have to check with them. You say he took one of the pills here, and the packet was already unwrapped as if he had at least examined them before coming in?"

"That's right, Inspector," said Mr. Wooderson. "I saw him take one of the pills. Later he came down from the Crusader Room saying something about having left the flipping pills in his coat pocket."

"And you don't think he had left them there?"

Mr. Wooderson scratched his head. "I'm almost sure I saw him put the box back in his waistcoat pocket, sir."

"Which is where they were found," said Knollis. "He and Morley were talking business?"

"So Cartland said. He was his usual bumptious self when they went up, but both were quiet and preoccupied when they came down about an hour and a quarter later."

"Sounds as if it was really serious business!"

"There's a thing I'd like to mention, Inspector."

"Let's have it."

"When the Super told me this morning that Cartland had been poisoned I was a bit worried in case it was something picked up here, so I checked with the wife. She bought the fish from a stall in the market, and saw it unloaded from a lorry which had come straight in from Grimsby, so that should have been fresh! Then I asked her how much the two had eaten, and what was left. She had to think it out, but eventually remembered that Morley had cleared the deck but for the sauce. Cartland left a completely clean plate. She mixed the sauce herself, and knows the stuff was all right because she'd used the same ingredients for several lunches she served."

"Well?"

"Mr. Cartland was the one with the tummy trouble."

"Yes?" Knollis prompted him gently.

"I know what I'm trying to say, but I've never been too handy with words."

"Suspicious of Mr. Morley? Is that it?"

"Something like that, Inspector. Somebody could have tampered with the food, couldn't they? Both men were in the room when my wife served the fish, and it was after that when Mr. Morley came down to use the telephone, and after *that* when Mr. Cartland came down for his pills."

"You're trying to establish the innocence of food served by your wife," said Knollis.

"Yes, and I'm honest about it. What I'm trying to say is that Mr. Morley could have put something into Mr. Cartland's sauce while *he* was down—or the same thing could have happened the other way round."

Mr. Wooderson broke off and scratched his head.

"I'm getting bewildered," he said. "It was Mr. Morley who left the sauce, and Cartland who ate the lot!"

Knollis grinned. He was always amused by the strenuous efforts of amateur detectives. He decided to bewilder Mr. Wooderson still further.

"There's another angle you haven't thought out," he said earnestly. "Suppose Mr. Cartland doped Morley's sauce while he was down on the phone, and Morley realised it and switched plates while Cartland was downstairs in the cloak-room?"

Mr. Wooderson took the suggestion seriously. He whistled softly, and nodded several times. "That really raises something, Inspector!"

"I could raise a glass of mild-and-bitter if you'll draw me one, Mr. Wooderson," said Knollis.

Mr. Wooderson fetched two glasses. "On the house, sir. Cheerio!"

"There's yet a further possibility," said Knollis with the blandest of expressions. "Suppose the pills were poisoned!"

He smiled at the wondering landlord, and added: "Cheer up, Mr. Wooderson! I shouldn't tell you this, but I will, if only to relieve your anxieties. Whenever Cartland took the poison, it was before he came into your house at twenty minutes past six last night. The majority of the aconite which killed him was in his intestines. The meal you served was still in his tummy."

Mr. Wooderson gaped, and blew a deep breath. "The house is clear of all suspicion?"

"The house is clear," said Knollis, "and you needn't work your brains to death with further detective work. That's my job!"

Knollis emptied his glass, went up to this room for a wash, and went out into the busy streets, one hand jingling the bunch of keys he had adroitly borrowed from the tray of Cartland's belongings.

He walked to Pilgrim Corner, and looked at Cartland's shop, with its three huge windows over which the roller shutters were locked, and the deep entrance porch with its full length venetian glass panel. There was also a lattice-grilled gate, but this was folded back against the inner window.

He let himself in, and found himself facing a startled young woman, a pretty young woman in her middle twenties, neat in a brown dress with lace cuffs and collar which emphasised the blondness of her short-cut hair.

"Sorry!" said Knollis with a smile. "I didn't think anyone would be here. I'm Inspector Knollis, of the Yard."

She patted her heart. "You really scared me for a moment! I'm Norah Shawbrook, Mr. Cartland's manageress. I was just trying to sort out some figures for Mrs. Cartland. She's rather anxious to know how the business was run."

"She isn't the only one," murmured Knollis. Louder, he said: "You know you mustn't remove any account book or ledgers until we've been through them? So you are Miss Shawbrook, are you? Mrs. Cartland mentioned you to me."

He noticed a mark on the third finger of her right hand, a deep one suggesting she had worn a ring on it for a considerable period.

"Worked here long?" he asked casually.

"Just over six months, Inspector."

"Like it?"

She grimaced. "I've had worse! It isn't a bad one, really. It's clean, and Mr. Cartland paid me well, which was the main item."

Knollis lifted her hand and looked at the finger. "*Miss* Shawbrook?"

"My husband left me some time ago."

"Not a native of this district, are you?" asked Knollis. "Could I guess Surrey—or Sussex? Somewhere south of the Thames?"

"Richmond," she said shortly. "I came north to—to get away from people who knew me."

"These domestic tragedies are sad," murmured Knollis, shaking his head. "However, I haven't come to pry into your private life, have I? I'd like to look around the premises. Do a good trade here?"

"An excellent one, Inspector."

Knollis eyes the girl carefully. She was a confident, self-possessed young woman, and her chin showed a considerable amount of determination. She was very blonde—until you looked closely at the roots of her hair, which betrayed the use of a bleach. It was a very interesting fact.

Conscious of his scrutiny, Miss Shawbrook suddenly turned and led the way through a green-painted doorway. "This is the office," she said hastily.

"You do the books?"

"Oh yes, I'm general factotum around here."

"Nice room to work in," said Knollis. He nodded towards another open doorway at the far side of the room. "What's through there?"

"A short passage leading to the stairs. You'd like to go through the premises?"

"That's the general idea," Knollis assured her.

The first flight of stairs led to a long landing. Three doors opened from it, two leading to empty rooms, and the third to a well-filled stock-room. A second flight led to a similar landing on which were two more empty rooms, and one with a locked door.

"Have you a key?" asked Knollis.

Miss Shawbrook shook her head. "I've never even seen in this room, Inspector. In fact I can't remembering coming on this landing at all!"

"Really!" murmured Knollis.

He took Cartland's keys from his pocket and found one that fitted the lock. He threw open the door and walked in, followed by Miss Shawbrook. There was a long, lead-covered bench under the effacing windows. Over it, fixed to the wall, was a tool rack fitted with a variety of small screwdrivers, pliers, tiny saws, and a caliper gauge. On the bend were two crucibles, a Bunsen burner, and a gas ring fed by a rubber tube attached to a gas point on the wall.

"Mr. Cartland did his watch repairs here?"

Miss Shawbrook was staring wide-eyed round the room.

"N-no! We sent them all away, Inspector."

"No idea what's in the big safe?"

"I've never been up here before!"

"Oh no! I remember you saying so," said Knollis quietly. "I think we should look in the safe, don't you?"

Miss Shawbrook licked her lips and nodded mutely. Knollis again inspected the bunch of keys, and thrust one of them into the lock. He pulled back the heavy door.

"Hm!" he said.

"Aladdin's cave!" exclaimed Miss Shawbrook.

Knollis had to admit that the interior of the safe looked like it. It was fitted with shelves, and on them rested necklaces, bracelets, bangles, a coronet, cardboard boxes literally filled with gems and dozen roughly cast ingots of gold. A nice little collection!

"Mr. Cartland bought old gold!" he said sarcastically.

"Yes, but Mr. Cartland never bought *that* over the counter!" said Miss Shawbrook, taking him seriously.

"That's true," said Knollis. He pulled on his kid gloves and took the coronet from the safe. "Know who once wore that? It was worn at the last coronation, and the owner hoped to wear it at Queen Elizabeth's, too, but someone stole it. This necklace once belonged to the Duchess of Melborough—nice job, isn't? Here, let me see how you look in it!"

He threw the long necklace over Miss Shawbrook's head and then placed the coronet on her blonde curls at a rakish angle. He grinned at her. "You'd better slip downstairs and see how pretty you look in the mirror—and remember to come back!"

Miss Shawbrook stood silent, fingering the pearls.

Knollis racked his memory, and then took a bangle and three rings from the safe. He gently put them on the girl's fingers, and turned her around. "It might be the last time in your life that you'll be able to look like a duchess! Off you go!"

She suddenly turned and gave him a wistful smile. "All right, Inspector! Every girl dreams of such a moment!"

She ran lightly down the stairs, and Knollis took another look at the safe.

Miss Shawbrook came back bright-eyed. "You're a funny man for a policeman—and the papers always say—" She put her hand over her mouth. "Oh, I'm sorry!"

Knollis smiled. "They say I'm stodgy! I know that, Miss Shawbrook. Perhaps I'd better get back to my normal self. Ever heard of a man called Davidson?"

She looked curiously at him. "You mean the man Mr. Cartland sent to prison?"

"You can put it that way."

"I've heard Mr. Cartland speak of him, but it all happened before I came to Burnham."

Knollis gave her a cigarette, and lit it for her. "Anything queer, or unusual, ever happen on these premises? You know, anything that has surprised you in a respectable shop?"

"Well, only the parcels that came by carrier."

"Go on."

"In the normal way of things Mr. Cartland used to let me unpack new consignments, but there were some smaller ones, each marked with a large green cross in crayon, which he took to the office, and I never saw them again."

"Delivered by carrier."

"From London, Inspector."

Knollis looked sadly at the safe. "I'm afraid your interesting collection will have to be replaced, Miss Shawbrook, and then I'll lock up again and leave you to your more lawful occupations."

When she had closed the shop door behind him he stood for a few seconds with a wry smile on his lean face.

"Mrs. Shardlow," he said softly. "You're a very plucky little woman!"

CHAPTER V
DETECTIVES GALORE

MANSON SPRAWLED across his desk and flicked a spent match across the room. "So Roger Cartland was a fence!"

"To say the least of it," said Knollis.

"One of our most respected citizens," Manson said bitterly.

"I think I see the set-up in my mind's eye," said Knollis. "A mob has been operating south of London for some years, and we haven't been able to get a single line on them. Now, assume that Davidson was one of the mob. We know he was opening up on his own account, not being satisfied with the terms he was getting. Just imagine that he wanted to get rid of the Salisbury stuff in a hurry, and the gang are looking for a chance to shop him. He gets to know about Cartland in some way, probably being told by some bright boy that while Cartland isn't a fence within the meaning of the act he isn't too particular. Davidson falls for the story, and Cartland shops him when in possession of some good stuff."

Manson smiled. "Cartland is a good citizen, doing his duty by the community, and Davidson learns that he either plays ball with the gang or goes down the line again on a framed charge."

"Which means Cartland was a member of the organisation," added Knollis.

"The breaker-upper and disposer."

"I'm not so sure about him being the disposer," said Knollis. "If you saw the amount of stuff in his safe you'd think he was saving it against his own coronation. However, thinking it over, a somewhat weird idea has come into my head. I get 'em, you know!"

"Don't we all!"

"His partner's a goldsmith?"

"And silversmith."

"You don't understand what I'm getting at. What I'm asking is if he sells stuff other than he makes?"

"Oh no, he's purely what he says he is, a craftsman working to orders. The best job he's done up to now is the silver-gilt cruet which Old Puffing presented to the City Plate when his term as Lord 'Mur' was over—the ignorant old so-and-so. Worst Tory I've ever met."

Knollis smiled. "It could be funny!"

Manson cocked an enquiring eye. "What could?"

"If the silver-gilt cruet made for the retiring chief magistrate of the city was made with stuff melted down by Cartland."

Manson sat bolt upright, and then hurriedly shuffled round as the cigarette fell from his lips and rolled between his jacket and his pullover. He recovered it, brushed the sparks away, and whistled softly.

"Whew-hew! It could be! It could be at that!"

"But how the devil do we get into Morley's workshops to compare the ingots with those in Cartland's safe? We haven't a shred of an excuse."

"Have to think out a wangle," said Manson.

"Know the local newspaper people? Yes, of course you do, and that was a silly question. Which is the magaziney one? The—er—what's it called?"

"*Weekly Echo*. Twelve pages of local features, with pictures, the odd short story, an article or two by local would-be writers who can't write, and that kind of thing. Very parish magaziney. Pauley, the editor, is keen on encouraging local talent, and to be perfectly honest, while he's published a lot of tripe he's given a handful of promising writers the encouragement to keep going."

"He's the man we want," said Knollis. "Let's go to see him."

Mr. Pauley was a short man, natty, smart, and businesslike Knollis and Manson had to take him into their confidence, but knew they could rely on him. Manson knew him personally, and Knollis relied on his own knowledge of human nature.

"I can help you," he said when the tale was told. "I'm starting a feature series dealing with Burnhamites who have brought credit to the town. I know a good freelance who could interview Morley, and be shown round the workshops. Perhaps you'd like photographs as well?"

Knollis put his hands on his knees and leaned forward. "How long have you had this series in mind, Mr. Pauley?"

"Every second of two minutes, Inspector! Now let me be honest. I'm an editor before I'm a police co-operator. You'll allow me to publish the article, and later bring off a scoop but telling the true story? That's a bargain?"

"It's a bargain," said Knollis. "You'll wait for our signal before going ahead?"

"Naturally," Mr. Pauley replied. "Now the woman I have in mind is Mrs. Buell, a very active red-head who always gets what she wants once she's made up her mind that she wants it."

"That says everything," said Manson; "and a bit more besides!"

"How much will we have to tell her?" asked Knollis.

"All of it!" Mr. Pauley said firmly.

"This week's *treemen-dous* true confession," said Manson. "Next week it will be the story of Molly Malone, the Girl Who Left Ireland. Read all about her inside."

"How soon can we see her?" asked Knollis.

"Her inside?" asked Manson, who seemed pleased with his joke.

"Mrs. Buell!"

"I'll telephone her now," said Mr. Pauley, "and have her come straight into the office. She runs a small car she's bought with her earnings as a free-lancer."

"We're in the wrong profession," said Knollis.

Mr. Pauley nodded as he replaced the receiver. "She'll be here in twenty minutes. Now I'll fix an appointment with Mr. Morley."

"And if he won't play?" asked Manson.

"It's my business to encourage people to play," Mr. Pauley said with an optimistic smile. "You sit back and listen, Super!"

He certainly had a persuasive tongue. Mr. Morley was apparently reluctant to consider any feature dealing with himself while his partner's death was being investigated.

"Mr. Cartland would have jumped at it," said Mr. Pauley, "and I know only too well that if he were still with us he would recommend you to accept this free publicity we are offering. Neither Mr. Cartland nor the manner of his death will be mentioned in the article, and we *do* want to open with a really good subject like yourself!"

He winked at Knollis and Manson, and listened. Morley finally agreed to receive Mrs. Buell, her notebook, pencil, and camera at three that afternoon, and metaphorically waved away Mr. Pauley's apologies for this terribly short notice.

Mrs. Buell proved to be as vivacious and mentally alert as Mr. Pauley had described her.

"We don't want to do anything melodramatic such as swearing you to secrecy," said Knollis, "but we must be able to rely on your absolute discretion. Now here's the story . . ."

Mrs. Buell licked her lips as Knollis told her what he wanted her to do. She obviously relished the assignment given to her.

"Now if I may use your telephone, Mr. Pauley?"

He rang the shop on Pilgrims Corner, and nodded his satisfaction on receiving no reply. He took Manson and Mrs. Buell with him to the shop, and showed them the interior of the safe on the second floor with the showmanship of an amateur conjurer producing his first rabbit from a hat.

"There!" he said. "Ever see anything like that outside the Tower of London?"

Manson shook his head. "Only in jewellers' windows!"

"I'd love to write an article on it," said Mrs. Buell, licking her lips hungrily.

"That's the easiest way to get an inside story about Gabthorpe Prison," said Knollis.

She leaned negligently against the safe and smiled winningly at Knollis. "When the case is over . . ."

"I think you could go as far as a magazine article. Mr. Vivian might object if you started writing a book about it."

"Yes, of course," she said understandably. A lovely title! *Inspector Knollis calls Open Sesame!*"

"For the time being," said Knollis, we'd prefer you to concentrate on the ingots—like these. The rest is obvious."

"You think Mr. Morley—but perhaps I'd better not say it?"

"I think that would be wise, Mrs. Buell!" said Knollis. He got rid of her by escorting her down the stairs and closing the shop door firmly behind her.

"I only hope we haven't let too many people in, he said when he rejoined Manson upstairs.

"I'm looking at these ingots," said Manson. "They're an amateurish job, and I can't help thinking that if Morley had been in the game he'd have done this part of the job, and they wouldn't have been so crude. Oh, and what's in the cupboard in the corner?"

Knollis opened it with a key from Cartland's ring. It produced a set of home-made moulds, and several dozen sheets of wrapping-paper, each used, and each bearing the house label of a firm of London bullion dealers: *G.S. Washington & Co.* Each bore a large green cross, drawn on it with crayon.

"A job for the blokes back at the Yard," said Knollis. "We'll have them check on consignments from Washington. Now suppose we lock up and go down to look at the books?"

Manson was fingering the pearl necklet. "I don't profess to be a memory man, but if those pretties didn't belong to the Duchess of Melborough you can chase me around the block."

"You won't get chased," Knollis assured him. "They did! The Madison Flats job. But I can't tell you all that went missing. We'll have to get Burnell down to check 'em over."

They collected Cartland's ledgers and took them back to headquarters, to find Sir Edmund Griffin waiting for them in Manson's office. He threw a small pill-box on the table and shook his head. "Innocent as new-born lambs. Pure as the dew. Nothing but herbs in them—plus the gelatin and sugar coatings, of course!"

"Which means—" said Manson.

"Another good idea gone down the drain," said Knollis. "Somehow we have to find where he went between leaving the Thursday luncheon and arriving at the Spaniels, and between leaving Morley at the shop and crashing down the slope of Locksley Vale."

He opened the box and looked thoughtfully, almost regretfully, as the remains of the pills. "I could have sworn they were responsible!"

Sir Edmund shrugged. "If you disbelieve my analysis you can always send them down to the forensic people!"

Knollis laid the box on the table. "Your reputation's good enough for me, Sir Edmund. Damn it, nevertheless!"

"How is the case progressing?" Sir Edmund asked.

"Slowly," replied Knollis. "We've searched Cartland's place on Pilgrim Corner, and there's no doubt that he was a fence. Thanks for the tip!"

"Interviewed Morley yet?"

"No, we're waiting a few hours until certain investigations are complete. We have the net out for Davidson—we'd dearly like a talk with him."

Sir Edmund took a small diary from his pocket. "He's lodging at Twenty-four Harwood Square. His present name is Dalton, and he's a commercial traveler selling a new ball-point pen."

Knollis raised an eyebrow. "How the deuce did you get hold of that dope?"

"Ignatius, of course," sighed Sir Edmund. "The little man knows everything. I almost suspect that he knows the identity of Cartland's killer. He is still trying to prove Shardlow's innocence, and also watching you very closely. He says you will inevitably become suspicious of certain innocent people, and it is his duty to protect him."

"Complimentary, I must say," snorted Knollis. "Where is Ignatius living?"

"At a pub in Locksley, the Ram and Crook. And now I must go, having another appointment."

Knollis watched him go, and turned to Manson with a twisted smile. "This should prove interesting—we two, our men, plus four amateurs."

Manson ticked them off on his fingers. "Old Griffin, this Brother Ignatius, Pauley, and Mrs. Buell, eh? You're asking Super Burnell to come down, and have two sergeants present checking with Washingtons—or will have when you've been on the blower!"

"I'll do that now," said Knollis.

"And I'll be glad when Mrs. Buell has done her stuff," said Manson. "I'm most interested in her antics."

Ms. Buell presented herself at five o'clock, and handed over her camera, which was rushed to the photographic department.

"Those gold bars were identical with the ones you showed me in Mr. Cartland's safe," she reported. "There were half a dozen of them in a strong-room built into a cellar under the shop. There are two keys. One is kept in the safe in the office attached to the shop, and he carries the other with him. I had some trouble getting him to let me photograph the strong-room, but I insisted that Mr. Pauley wanted to be able to produce a series of snaps showing the whole process from gold bars to finished work. He wanted to know who else was featuring in the series, and I had to hatch up some names on the spot—which means Mr. Pauley will have to let me do them now. Three guineas a time! Hurrah!"

She waited with them until wet prints were brought in, and she had been congratulated on them. She was then given her camera and allowed to depart. Actually, she had to be pushed from the room, being more interested than Knollis wanted her to be.

"Now what have we got?" asked Manson. He put his feet up on the desk and slid lower in his chair. "What have we got, and where do we go from here?"

"A case against Morley," Knollis replied.

Manson glanced curiously at him. "But you said that if Morley had been in at the game he would surely have done the casting of the ingots."

"I did," said Knollis. "That isn't the angle."

He strode across the room and took his hat and coat from the pegs. "Let's have a chat with him."

Joseph Pevensey Morley was distinctly nervous in their presence. He chewed a cigarette until it had to be thrown away, and then he played with the end of his tie, rolling it and unrolling it until it looked like a piece of corrugated cardboard.

"You must have known Cartland very well," said Knollis. "Was his business run straight? Was he an honest man?"

Morley seemed reluctant to answer. "Well, Superintendent Manson knew him well enough!"

"I wasn't his partner," Manson pointed out. "I merely knew him as one of several thousand Burnham shopkeepers."

"Will it help," asked Knollis, "if we say we believe Roger Cartland to have been a fence—a receiver of stolen property?"

"A—a receiver of stolen property?" Morley stammered.

"Let's be done with the play-acting," said Knollis. "There's something like ten thousand pounds' worth of stolen jewellery in a safe in an upper room at Pilgrim Corner."

He saw that Morley was shaken, and pressed his advantage. "You did know, didn't you? You were aware of the fact! You knew he was an out-and-out rogue!"

"Ye-es," Morley admitted lamely. "I found out quite recently."

"And that was the mater you discussed at the Spaniels!"

"Yes, that's right, Inspector."

"Care to tell us about it, voluntarily?"

Morley flopped heavily on a bentwood chair, and clasped his hands tightly between his knees. He stared miserably at the floor. "I thought all along that there was a catch in it, but he always seemed so open and honest. Then, you see, I began to have real doubts. He ran the business end, and ordered all them materials. He said he could make sharper deals that I could, and every shilling added up by the end of the year."

"He supplied you with the metals you used in the workshop?" asked Manson.

Knollis trod heavily on his toes.

Morley looked up. "If you know that, you must know the rest. It was only because I am a craftsman that I caught him out. It was the gold. It isn't all one colour, you know, not in the raw. African gold is reddish, and the rare Welsh gold is almost white, and there are dozens of variations in between. Roger couldn't have known that, and the stuff he was sending to me was useless for fine work. I challenged him, and told him frankly what I suspected. He dared me to expose him. He said nobody would believe I wasn't his partner in that as well as the business. I told him we couldn't carry on any longer, and a solution would have to be found. He told me to think about it for a few days, because if he went down the line he'd take me with him!"

"Yes?" murmured Knollis.

"That was ten days ago. After the Thursday luncheon he suggested dinner at the Spaniels, when we'd discuss the whole thing thoroughly. Mrs. Cartland was away from home, and he didn't feel like a lonely meal at home anyway. Well, we met there and went into the whole thing. I suggested that he should retire, and he said he'd retire over my dead body—and that was even before we sat down to dine! The conversation got hotter as it went on. He said he'd always wanted money, and the power it would give him. He'd been brought up in the slums, and now he could meet people who mattered on equal terms. He could nod to the Lord Mayor, and chat with the Lord Lieutenant, and the Chief Constable, and people like that. He said if I thought he was going to lose all that I was a bloody fool!"

"What did he suggest?" asked Manson.

"That I carry on alone, and forget all about what he was doing. I said that was called condoning an offence, and I'd be as guilty as he was. It ended in a stalemate. We went back to the shop, and he showed me his private books, trying to convince me that the game was safe and profitable. He tried to persuade met to join him."

"Where on earth did he keep his private books?" Knollis interrupted.

"There's a cupboard behind the safe, and the safe is on runners so you can pull it out. His secret ledgers are in there."

"Then what happened?"

"He said he wasn't feeling too good, but had an appointment to keep before he could go home. He took a couple of pills and a drink of water and said they should straighten him up. My car was in the garage for new brake-linings. I could have caught a bus home, but truth to tell I wanted a chance to be alone and think, so I went down to the shop—to here, and Roger said he'd pick me up later. I knew I couldn't keep going now I knew the truth about him, and I knew I couldn't afford to pack up and start all over again. Just didn't know what to do, so I stooged round the workshop trying to puzzle things out."

He looked up again, complete frankness in his light blue eyes. "It was a shock when Kathleen rang to tell me about his death, but I also experienced a great sense of relief, because I knew the thing was solved. I could keep quiet now, and that would save trouble for Kath and myself—and for Mrs. Cartland. We both like her, and one of my problems before Roger's death was trying to solve the thing without hurting her. So Roger's death solved everything."

"You stayed in the shop—how long?" asked Knollis.

"Oh, from about half-past eight until my wife rang."

"You telephoned nobody from the shop?"

"No, Inspector."

"Nobody called to see you?"

"They wouldn't know I was here. The shop was in darkness and the communicating door closed."

"Nobody rang you?"

"No."

"Where was Cartland's car parked when you came from his shop to here?"

"Just up St. Giles' Lane."

"I see," Knollis said thoughtfully. "So you've no alibi for all the hours between leaving Roger Cartland and boarding the homeward-bound bus?"

"Do I need one?" Morley asked indignantly.

"Well," Knollis said slowly, "you had an excellent motive for causing Cartland's death, hadn't you? You've said yourself that *his death solved everything*."

"Oh, my God!" exclaimed Morley, suddenly panic stricken.

"Exactly!" said Knollis.

CHAPTER VI
EVIDENCE CONFLICTING

KNOLLIS WAS HEAVY-EYED when he awoke at seven the next morning. He and Manson had stayed up until three o'clock, examining the secret account books for in the cupboard behind the safe. They had proved interesting and illuminating, and Knollis wondered why an astute man like Cartland should have provided such a wealth of evidence against himself and his confederates. It could be because of his mania for accounting for every shilling and penny that drifted towards him.

Cartland's brother-in-law, William Farthingale, had been the head of the organisation, with Cartland as junior partner. They 'ordinary members' represented the cream of London's underworld, and if a little care was taken there was no reason why a highly satisfactory bag should not be taken. That was not Knollis's assignment, so the books were packed off to the Yard.

He turned to his bed to find Mr. Wooderson standing beside him with a tray on which rested a cup of tea and a round typewriter ribbon box.

"Good morning!" Knollis said hazily. He wriggled into a sitting position, and screwed his eyes against the light streaming through the mullioned windows. "What's the—er—box?"

"The wife found it behind the radiator in the cloaks, Inspector. Just behind the peg where Mr. Cartland hung his coat."

"You've looked inside it?"

"Yes."

Knollis took the box and removed the lid. Inside were a few shreds of what might have parsnip, or turnip, or even monkshood root.

"How long could it have been there, Mr. Wooderson?"

"Not long. My wife puts a feather duster down the back of the radiator every morning. She missed yesterday with all the upset and so on, but she says she definitely dusted the morning before . . ."

"Thursday morning . . ."

"Yes, sir."

"And Mr. Morley left his tartare sauce."

"Yes, sir," Mr. Wooderson said stolidly.

Knollis pushed his hands through his hair and swung his legs out of bed. "You know, Mr. Wooderson, we're really getting somewhere with this case. I've never known one produce results so early. I don't think I'll be your guest much longer."

Mr. Wooderson gave a wry smile. "From your point of view I hope you're right, Inspector. You do think that stuff is monkshood root?"

Knollis laughed shortly. "I'll be the most disappointed man in Burnham if it isn't!"

"Your tea will be getting cold," said Mr. Wooderson.

"How many people have handled the box?"

"Myself, my wife, and now you."

"We'll have to have our finger-prints taken," said Knollis. "Careless of me! Still, I was not properly awake. You won't mind supplying your dabs?"

"It'll be an experience, Inspector."

"We always destroy them afterwards," said Knollis.

He knew he was talking for talking's sake, trying to stir his sleepy mind, trying to make his thoughts marshal themselves in something like a logical order. He reached for the bedside telephone, got the police headquarters, and asked for someone to come to the Spaniels to take three sets of dabs. Then he dismissed the landlord, and sipped his tea.

The case was going very nicely indeed! There were two possible solutions: either Cartland had tried to poison Morley, and somehow administered the dose to himself, or Morley deliberately poisoned Cartland as the best solutions for his problem—and in either case the culprit was trying rid himself of a dangerous partner.

A thought came to him. Both men had come downstairs from the Crusader Room.

He kicked his slippers pettishly. Cartland was the prime mover in both cases. Morley had been *sent* to the telephone by Cartland. Accept that inevitable fact, and a reconstruction was easy. Cartland sent Morley down to the telephone while he mixed the monkshood root in Morley's tartare sauce. Then he had gone downstairs to hide the box behind the radiator. Had Morley then suspected the truth, and switched plates?

"Oh, lord!" Knollis said aloud. "Robins said he couldn't have taken the poison here! Then why the play-acting?"

He stared absently at the leaping blue flames of the gas-fire which Mr. Wooderson had lit before he awoke him. There *was* a degree of poison in Cartland's stomach, and it was the *main* dose that had passed down to his more intimate pipes! He had taken *two* doses. One at the Spaniels, and another some time previously.

He lay back on the bed for a while, and then again took up the bedside telephone, and lazily asked Mr. Wooderson, who had now taken the extension off the main line, to find Sir Edmund Griffin's number and call him.

Three minutes later Sir Edmund's housekeeper was protesting that Sir Edmund was in his bath.

"This is Detective-Inspector Knollis. I must speak to Sir Edmund at once."

There was another wait, and then Sir Edmund's querulous voice sounded in the receiver. "What the blazes do you want at this time of the day, Knollis. I was lazing in my bath!"

"Time you were up and working, like me," said Knollis, smiling secretly as he realised he was still in his pyjamas. "Listen, Sir Edmund, please. After that talk to the Locksley women, you went to Cartland's for a drink? That correct?"

"Correct, yes."

"Any idea how the conversation ran? Were any of the people—Cartland or his guests—interested in—well, more about the perfect murder?"

A deep sigh came over the wires. "Oh dear, I'll be in trouble again, but you may as well have the truth, Knollis. Cartland did ask if there were really any poisons unknown to science, as used by crime writers. I told him the truth; they did not exist—but on the other hand there were common poisons that were difficult to detect."

"Mentioning aconite, and monkshood," said Knollis gravely.

"Er—yes!"

"What did Cartland say to that?"

"He said he had monkshood in his garden, and would grub it all out and burn it. I told him he might have to burn at least half of garden if he took that attitude, since even the humble rhubarb leaves contained a quantity of oxalic acid, while poisons of the digitalis group could be obtained from the common foxglove. I seem to remember I mentioned Glaser's comments on the lily-of-the-valley, and how a girl in Germany was poisoned by the introduction of a distillation into her bedside glass of water."

"So!" said Knollis. "Thanks, Sir Edmund!"

He rang off before Sir Edmund had time to say more. So Cartland was primed in the use of aconite!

He shaved, washed, and dressed, and went down to breakfast. The sergeant had arrived to take the three sets of prints, and when that chore was done Knollis gave him the box in a large envelope and told him what to look for, Cartland's prints having been taken as he lay in the mortuary. He was also to tell Superintendent Manson that Inspector Knollis was going straight out to the Vale, and would return about half-past ten.

He was not satisfied in his own mind that Cartland had tried to murder Morley, and the tables had been turned on him either by accident or design. That accounted for the second and comparatively innocuous dose he had taken at the Spaniels. Now he had to trace the first, and fatal dose. The possibility existed that someone had entered Cartland's house and introduced the first dose into the horse-radish sauce made by the part-witted Gabby. Yes, that must be the answer! A substitution or introduction after the girl left for her home!

Knollis did justice to the excellent meal provided by Mrs. Wooderson, and at half-past eight drove out to the Vale. He went first to Gabby Jones's home, and learned from her mother that she arrived from Cartland's house at half-past three on the Thursday afternoon. He now had to trace the source of both doses, and with that in mind went to the cottage where lived the war-disabled man who tended Cartland's garden in his spare time.

"I'm a police-officer," he said, "and think you may be able to help me. Has monkshood ever been grown in Mr. Cartland's garden."

Derby, the gardener, changed his weight to his good leg, and nodded slowly. "Funny you should ask that, sir. Mr. Cartland had me dig it all out not more than a week ago. He said he hated the sight of it."

"What did you do with it?"

"Chucked it in the compost bin as Mr. Cartland said I should."

"The compost bin is kept—where?"

"Behind the greenhouse, sir."

"And this was about a week ago?"

"It would be—let me see—ay, last Friday. A week yesterday."

"Thanks," said Knollis. He gave the man a tip and went back to his car.

He drove to the Cartland house, left his car by the roadside, and went round the back of the house to the compost bin. He pulled on his gloves and began to empty the conglomeration of grass-cuttings, kitchen refuse, and garden refuse from the split-log bin. After delving a foot down he saw the serrated leaves of monkshood. He cleared the plants carefully, and decided that Sergeant Luck was working for him this day, for the plants were rootless.

He ambled into the greenhouse and looked round. At the end opposite the door he found several deep cuts, new ones, in the green-painted staging. He grubbed in the soil beneath and found half a dozen small chippings or slicings which he was sure the Forensic Laboratory would identify as monkshood root. He put them in an envelope, sealed it, and placed it in his wallet. He took the plants to the car and laid them on the rear seat. After them he threw his soiled gloves. He took a clean pair from his pocket, locked the car, and went up to the house.

Gabby told him that Mis' Car'land was busy, but he insisted on seeing her. She was fetched from the lounge, and Knollis asked her for a private word in her ear—preferably in the kitchen, if she didn't mind entertaining there.

"This is a little difficult, almost embarrassing," he said, scratching his ear. "Gabby told me she made horse-radish sauce for your husband last Thursday. Has she a private recipe, or have you taught her how to make it?"

"She uses my recipe book, Inspector. She can read, even if her thinking is below normal. In other words, she can obey instructions whether written or verbal."

"Can you give me a list of ingredients?"

Marion Cartland opened a drawer and produced a leather-bound recipe book. "Here is one I got from *Home & Country*—our W.I. magazine. Horse-radish, milk, sugar, mustard, salt, pepper, and vinegar."

"Where do you keep all those things?"

She opened a cupboard. Knollis pulled on his gloves and took down the bottle of vinegar, the mustard tin, and then looked round at Mrs. Cartland. "Would she use the pepper and salt from these tins, or from the cruet?"

"From the tins."

"Mind if I borrow them for the time being?"

Marion Cartland looked puzzled. "Obviously not, but—er—why?"

"I don't suppose there's any harm done in telling you," said Knollis. "He had tea at home last Thursday. Gabby left him a meal. And you know those facts. I'm wondering if someone came in the house and substituted monkshood sauce."

He laughed shortly. "I'm almost turning into a mystery-novel detective with my pre-occupation with fingerprints, but the fact remains that if we find only your own, and Gabby's, prints on the tins and the bottle I can dismiss the somewhat melodramatic idea from my mind. You won't object to having your dabs—fingerprints—taken?"

"No-o, I suppose not."

"I'll be back in a minute," said Knollis.

He carried his collection to the car, and returned with the murder bag, from which he took the fingerprint apparatus. Marion Cartland was visibly uncomfortable about the whole affair, but Gabby seemed to find it an excuse for a deal of wriggling and giggling.

"All this appears most horribly boring and unnecessary," Mrs. Cartland protested as she vigorously applied sink-powder to her ink-stained finger-tips. "Is the whole of our job so uninteresting—unromantic?"

Knollis smiled at her. "According to one self-styled critic I'm supposed to be the dullest detective in England. That's because I won't give sensational interviews to the Press, and allow my biographer to over-dramatise my performances. Romance exists in the lives and jobs of everybody but ourselves!"

"I—er—don't quite follow you, Inspector!" Marion Cartland said uncertainly.

"Don't you, Mrs. Cartland? That's a great pity. By the way, how is the conference progressing?"

"Conference?"

"Didn't I hear visitors in the lounge as Gabby showed me in? Perhaps the Morleys, and Miss Shawbrook?"

"Miss Shawbrook is staying with me for a few days. I told you yesterday I badly needed her help and advice with regard to the business!"

Knollis nodded. "She should be able to tell you a great deal. She, and Mr. Morley!"

"*Someone* has to help me. I never knew the first thing about Roger's business, and Mr. Manson and yourself have hardly helped me by confiscating all the books!"

"Sorry about that," said Knollis in an unconvincing voice. "We'll probably be able to return them tomorrow. We were merely checking in case he was being blackmailed."

"Blackmailed, Inspector! Roger!"

Marion Cartland was obviously very shocked by the suggestion.

"We don't suggest it, Mrs. Cartland. We don't even suspect it. But you never know, so we looked through his accounts to see if any queer and unexplained sums had been paid by him. We're satisfied now."

"That he wasn't being blackmailed, I hope!"

"That he wasn't, Mrs. Cartland."

"I should think not!" she said indignantly.

"But there was some reason, Mrs. Cartland!

She licked her lips. "Ye-es, of course. Yes, I appreciate that."

Knollis looked down at his shoes. "I wonder . . . ? Could I have a word with Mrs. Morley while I'm here? It would save a journey."

"I suppose so, Inspector. I'll ask her to step in. In here?"

"The kitchen will do quite well," said Knollis.

He packed the murder bag while she was away, and then took out his silver cigarette case and polished it with his handkerchief. He handled it by its edges, and laid it on the corner of the table after taking out one cigarette and sticking it in between in lips. When Kathleen Morley entered he was at the other side of the table, fastening his bag.

"Good Morning!" he smiled. "Help yourself to a cigarette while I finish this, Mrs. Morley!"

"Thanks!" she said cautiously. She took a cigarette and waited. Knollis came round the table with his lighter, and then picked up the case by its edges and dropped it in his pocket. The oldest and corniest trick in detective-dom had succeeded yet once more, and he was now in possession of a good set of Mrs. Morley's prints.

He lolled negligently against the table and looked at the burning end of his cigarette.

"There's a rather tricky point," he said, as if hesitant to state it. "Your husband was at the shop alone at the time Roger Cartland was driving to the Vale, and his death. We know you were in contact with him during that time—luckily for him! How many times did you telephone him during the course of the evening, Mrs. Morley?"

She looked at him for a few seconds, and then said: "Three, Inspector!"

"At what times?"

"Oh, at eight, nine, and then when I heard about Roger."

"Thanks so much," said Knollis. "That was all I needed to know—"

He stood erect as Morley entered the kitchen.

"Kathleen!"

"Well," she said carelessly; "what is it?"

"Oh, nothing!" he said, and lounged away again.

She turned, tight-lipped, to Knollis. "Why did you ask that question?"

Knollis drew the murder bag across the table and picked it up. "He told me that no one had phoned him during the evening, Mrs. Morley. That meant he had no alibi, and I thought you'd be inclined to supply him with one."

"Supply—supply him with an alibi? Why should Joe need an alibi? Why should he *need* one?"

Knollis smiled blandly. "You read, and study, crime fiction, Mrs. Morley. You should know that everyone needs an alibi. It's one of the rules of the game! But you're correct, of course! Why should he need an alibi? He was in town all evening, and Roger Cartland died in the Vale of Locksley. No, the world alibi is wrong, too loosely used. I should have asked you for corroboration of his statement. That was necessary, you know, since so far as we can learn your husband was the last person to see Roger Cartland alive."

Kathleen Morley let the cigarette drop from her fingers, and regardless of Mrs. Cartland's clean floor she screwed it into a black mess with the heel of her grey suede shoe.

"Where was Roger all that time?" she asked. "He left Joe at—oh, what about half-past eight! It couldn't have taken him an hour to drive home to the Vale. It wouldn't have taken that time even if he had been drunk?"

"Wouldn't it?" Knollis asked. "Have you tried it?"

"Oh!" she snapped. She walked round the kitchen, and faced him across the table. "What are you getting at, Inspector? Trying to pin the thing on Joe?"

Knollis shook his head. "No. You should know that, being a reader of authentic crime books. We don't do that kind of thing in England. No, Mrs. Morley, I want to know where both your husband and Roger Cartland were between half-past eight and the time of Cartland's death—which was approximately at half-past nine. Yes, at the time when he ran off the main road, *at right angles to the only gap in the wall for at least two miles—a gap that allows a bare three inches in clearance on each side!*"

Kathleen Morley grasped the edge of the table and said: "Oh!"

"Roger Cartland didn't drive through that gap, Mrs. Morley! He was driven through it—or the car was, if you're at all pernickety about the English language."

Morley re-entered the kitchen.

"What's going on here?" he demanded. "It sounds as if somebody is trying to bully my wife!"

"Nothing could be further from the truth," Knollis answered him mildly. "We were merely discussing telephone calls. You see, it is possible to check them . . ."

Morley flushed, and stammered unintelligibly for a few seconds.

"Well," he said brusquely when he had collected himself, "if that's all that's worrying you I can tell you the truth. Kathleen didn't ring me to tell me about Roger. She tried to do so, but I'd gone up to Pilgrim Corner to see if Roger was there. He wasn't, so I rang her from the call-box in St Giles' Lane. I rang Cartland's house first, so I rang Kathleen to tell her I'd have to catch the first bus home—which happened to be the last one as well."

"That's better," said Knollis. "It makes a much better story. Why didn't you tell me that at first?"

"Well . . ."

"Well?"

Morley shuffled uncomfortably. "Well, I just sort of answered as I thought. You asked me where I was and all that, and I said Kathleen told me over the phone."

"That's correct," said Knollis. "You did."

"It didn't seem necessary then to say whether I rang Kathleen, or whether she rang me. She told me about it, and that was the main thing."

"I quite understand," said Knollis. "We Britishers are inclined towards loose speech. As a rule it's in order—for all normal purposes, but in a murder investigation every word from a witness is of vital importance. Thanks for the explanations. I really must get back to town now," he said, as if the Morleys were detaining him.

"Where the deuce have you been?" Manson asked when Knollis walked into the office and laid his collection on the table.

"Playing a very old game, Manson. I've been making a woman suspicious of her husband, so suspicious that she'll badger him to death for the name of the blonde he was with."

"And if he wasn't with a blonde?"

"Then," Knollis said grimly, "he was pushing Roger Cartland, in his car, to his death! Now these things should go through to Dabs straight away . . ."

Manson looked wonderingly at Knollis. "What's the next move?"

"Night train to London, and thence to the Isle of Wight."

"You're going to see Shardlow?"

"That's the general idea," said Knollis.

CHAPTER VII
REVELATIONS OF THREE

ARTHUR SHARDLOW was a tall, plump man whose prison suit made him look anything but an ex-policeman. He stared moodily at the surface of the oak desk in the Governor's office, and was disinclined to talk.

"The Inspector is trying to help you, Shardlow," said the Governor.

"The time has come," said Knollis, "to talk of many things; of shoes, and ships, and sealing wax, and country-house robberies and such-like things. I've had a chat with Brother Ignatius, and I've read the report of your trial while on the way down."

"There's nothing to talk about," replied Shardlow. "I've had a fair trial, and that's that. I'm satisfied."

"Look, Galahad," said Knollis. "There's more to this case than your own bright ideas. We know for a fact that Roger Cartland is dead, having been neatly murdered, and I need all the help I can get if I'm to find his murderer. You were innocent of the job for which you were sentenced, and you won't solve it yourself if you stay here for another twenty years."

He paused, and added: "You know your wife has disappeared?"

"She's with friends in West Harrow. I get letters from here. She's all right, so you needn't drag her in!"

"She's in Burnham," Knollis said calmly, "Masquerading as Miss Shawbrook, and has been working as Cartland's manageress and secretary."

Shardlow looked up. "That's not true!"

"She's bleached and dyed her hair, shorn her eyebrows, and changed her style of dress—but she still resembles your wife."

"But she's—she's in danger!" Shardlow exclaimed.

Knollis nodded: "I thought you'd see the point."

"Where is she now? Now Cartland's dead?"

"Living with Mrs. Cartland for a fortnight, putting her wise to how the business was run—or how Mrs. Cartland will think it is run."

Shardlow shook his head. "I told her to keep out of it! It's no job for a woman. These men are dangerous."

"What's your story?" asked the Governor. "Let's have it out of you, Shardlow!"

"How much did you know about Farthingale and Cartland?" asked Knollis.

He offered Shardlow a cigarette. It was his third in twenty minutes, and he was practically eating them. He took it with a muttered word of thanks and lit it from the stub of the near-finished one.

"I don't know how it started, not for sure," he said slowly. "There was a suspicion here, and one there, and then I twice saw a doubtful-looking character dodging into Farthingale's grounds. No, it was built up on seemingly insignificant items. Then there was a peculiar incident one day when I was standing in a field gateway to have a crafty smoke. A carrier's van drew up outside Farthingale's main gates, and the driver collected a parcel from the van and walked up the drive with it. As soon as he was out of sight the odd character I'd seen came out of the hedge, took a parcel from the van, and put another one in. He put the one from the van in the hedge-bottom, and walked up the road towards me. I leaned over the gate and tried to look as if I'd seen nothing, and as if I was hiding my cigarette. He came up and asked for a light. I asked a few questions, and he said he came from Cranston, and was walking to Canterbury to

see about a job—getting lifts when he could. He had an introduction card from the Labour Exchange, and means of providing his identity. He had money with him, and so I'd nothing on
him—apart from what I'd seen. Acting on a hunch, I let him go. I
collected the parcel and took it home with me. It was addressed
to Roger Cartland, Pilgrim Corner, Burnham, and contained a
dozen alarm clocks. I sealed it up again and took it down to the
station as found on the roadside, having apparently fallen from
a lorry. I learned later than no parcels were missing from the
van, and it was presumed that some packer had made a mistake,
and its falling from the van was pure coincidence.

"Where was the parcel sent from?"

"Lewes. Farthingale has an interest in a firm there."

"All very roundabout, surely?" mused Knollis.

"You know more about the criminal mind than I do, sir," said
Shardlow. "Don't they always over-complicate their plans? Isn't
that were they always slip?"

"That's true enough," Knollis agreed readily. "From Lewes to
Lonsdale, from there to London, and on to Burnham. Farthingale daren't send the stuff direct, of course. Anyway, what's your
next move?"

"I kept an eye on Farthingale. He seemed to go out a great
deal with the car, apparently touring aimlessly round the countryside. I got two friends to help me in checking him. Over a
period of months we discovered that if Farthingale went to, say,
Brighton on the first day of the month there was a breaking job
there in the next dark-moon period. I was just getting the thing
down to a system when they framed me—and I fell for it like a
ripe apple!"

"What was your plan?"

"To find them on the job, ring the station, and catch them at
work. Instead of which—but you know the story, sir."

"Why the hell did you accept the accusation?" asked the
Governor.

Shardlow ran his hand through his har. "I was wrong, but I
thought a spell in stir would give me the rest of the information I

wanted. As a policeman gone wrong I could gain the confidence of some of the old lags."

"They won't play?"

Shardlow shook his head. "Candidly, sir, I'm having a rough time. I think they all know the truth, and suspect me of being a stool-pigeon, and the whole affair as a job sponsored by the Yard."

"You're ready to come out?"

"I am after what you've told me about my wife."

Knollis pushed his cigarettes across the table. Heard anything about Gentleman Davidson while you've been here?"

"He's for it!" said Shardlow. "He should emigrate—in fact I've heard that he's going to do so. He's given the go-by to what the pirates used to call the Articles of Agreement. They shopped him by sending him to Cartland, of course. Cartland was waiting for him."

"He's packing up?"

"When he's squared his account with Cartland."

"He's said that?"

"So the boys say," said Shardlow, nodding his head in the general direction of the cell blocks. "He's fallen for some blonde or other . . ."

His voice trailed away, and he stared wonderingly at Knollis and the Governor.

"Hey! What *is* happening?"

Knollis was several paces ahead of him, but remained silent, hoping Shardlow would tell him more than he knew.

"What is happening?" asked the Governor.

"It's my wife who's stringing him along!

"True," said Knollis.

"Then it was she who sent him to Cartland!"

"I suspected it," said Knollis, nodding like a mandarin doll.

"But—but I don't get it!"

"Your wife's a single-minded person, what is generally known as a one-man dog."

"She certainly is!"

"Can't you follow the sequence of her thoughts?" asked Knollis. "She read your notes, heard what little you had told her, put two and two together, and went to work. After all, no woman likes to see her husband go to prison! She sought out Davidson and gained his confidence. His job happened after yours, didn't it?"

"Yes. You know that!"

"Your wife set out to bring down the gang single-handed. All police wives know something of the law. Village police wives know a great deal as a rule, since they are virtually acting-station-sergeants when their husbands are out on patrol. So she sent Davidson to Cartland, knowing Cartland would shop him— it was a pretty shrewd guess, anyway. Then when Davidson came out she had an ally. She then go the job with Cartland— and how she got it beats me! She got the job so that she could get direct internal evidence."

"Then it was Davidson who—"

Knollis interrupted him. "Davidson didn't murder Cartland, if that's what you're thinking. He wasn't in town that day. I don't think so, that is."

He sucked a tooth, and looked cautiously at Shardlow. "Aren't we perhaps jumping to a conclusion about it being your wife Davidson has fallen for?"

"I don't think so, sir. I was told he'd picked up a blonde who lived at Lonsdale. He dropped across her somewhere in London, and the description was, now I think about it, a good one but for the colour of the hair. That puzzled me, because I couldn't think of a Lonsdale blonde likely to have teamed up with a man like Davidson. After all, it was my village, and I thought that I knew all the characters!"

Knollis sighed. "Fair enough, Mr. Shardlow. You can go and change into your civvy suit. I've fixed things with the Yard and the Home Office, and you're returning to Burnham with me. You can either come on your word of honour, or in cuffs. Please yourself. If you come as a free man you're under my strict orders. Otherwise, a warder accompanies us."

"You have my word, sir."

"You'll have a room at the Spaniels Inn, where I'm lodging, and you'll have to keep to it. You see, I'm lighting the fuse and blowing the whole thing sky-high when we get back."

The governor pressed a bell-push, and a warder entered to take charge of Shardlow. An hour later they left the prison in a closed car and started the journey to Burnham. A curtained car was waiting at Burnham Victoria Station, and Knollis took Shardlow straight to the Spaniels, warning the Woodersons to know nothing of the man in the next room to himself, but to feed him well. He went on to police headquarters to report to the Chief Constable and Manson.

He told his story fully, and asked for the local news.

"You," said the Chief Constable, nodding to Manson.

"A quiet two days," said Manson. "Dabs found a jumble of prints on the poison box—yours, Wooderson's, and Cartland's only."

"The kitchen equipment from Locksley?"

"Those of the daft maid, and Mrs. Cartland's. No more."

"Mrs. Shardlow still out at the Cartland house?"

"Yes. She's given up her flat."

"I see," said Knollis. "I think we should have a conference. Send out a car for Mrs. Shardlow—as Miss Shawbrook, and have Davidson collected. You've had him under observation?"

"All the time. Don't you worry about that! Having a shut-down, eh?"

"It should clear the decks," said the Chief Constable.

The conference was held in Mr. Wooderson's large saloon on the first floor. Mrs. Shardlow was brought in first, and shown the sitting-room. She had not been warned of her husband's presence in Burnham, so that she walked into the room, stared, and fled sobbing into her husband's arms. Knollis discreetly walked to the window and kept his back towards them for several minutes before breaking up the party. He turned back into the room smiling at them. "I'll give you a few minutes later," he said. "We have work to do now.

Mrs. Shardlow wiped her tears away, and fumbled in her bad for her compact. "How—how did you know, Inspector?" she faltered.

"I'm a detective," he said dryly. "And there's only one thing I want to say before I take you into this conference we're holding, and that is you've both finished with detecting! Whether your husband finishes his sentence depends entirely upon yourselves. Now please come this way."

He led them into the room where the Chief Constable, Manson, Lawton, and Dr. Robins were waiting. In the next hour they sorted out the tangled tale which had been privately investigated by Shardlow and his wife. Superintendent Burnell joined them halfway through the conference and supplied a few of the pieces from his own experience.

"There's no doubt about it," he said; "Farthingale was master-mind. He did all the initial research and planning, and detailed the men for each job. We've now got their names, and those of the go-betweens. The stuff was switched exactly as Shardlow has described, but not always at Lonsdale. It came on to Cartland, who broke it up and disposed of it. Cartland also bought old gold, so some of it was put in with that, and sent to the bullion dealers in the normal manner. I've relayed all this to the Yard, and the whole mob will be picked up tonight. The murder is Inspector Knollis's affair, and I'm not interfering there, but as I see it his best bet is Mr. Joseph Pevensey Morley, who either poisoned Cartland deliberately, or twisted an attempt by Cartland to poison him. You pays your pennies, you takes your choice."

"Now let's have Davidson in," said Knollis.

Gentleman Davidson entered in a grand manner that had earned him his nickname. He was slight of build, neatly dressed, and close-shaven except for a trim military moustache which he constantly fingered. He wore a carnation in the button-hole of his grey lounge suit, and generally tried to look as if he was in surroundings which were below his social standing.

"Take a pew," said Knollis. "We're holding you for questioning—and how long depends on yourself. In any case you'll be staying with us until Mr. Farthingale and his friends are safely inside."

Davidson raised an eloquent eyebrow. "You've got them all? Good work!"

"They'll be inside by nightfall" said Knollis.

"You make sure Willie doesn't get out of Lonsdale village," said Davidson with a knowing nod. "He has a private airfield in the name of John Stowe not five miles from his home, and a single-engined cabin plane ready for a take-off night or day. That's how he got the gems to Holland."

"Well, I'll be damned!" exclaimed Shardlow.

Davidson smiled. "Even the village copper was deceived, eh?"

"Excuse me," said Burnell, and bustled from the room demanding the use of the telephone.

"Thanks for that information," said Knollis. "Now perhaps you'd care to tell your story?"

"That depends," said Davidson. "I've retired from an illicit business, and fail to see why I should run myself into quod again. By the way, why is Miss Shawbrook here?"

Knollis looked round at the embarrassed girl. "Care to introduce yourself? No? Meet Mrs. Shardlow, Davidson. Wife of the village constable of Lonsdale."

Davidson looked across at her, and sniffed. "Serves me jolly well right! Never trust a woman. Oh, well . . . !"

"Your story," said Knollis.

"You know the first part of it, Inspector. I came back to Burnham with the intention of relieving Mr. Cartland of the exact amount he owed me for the Salisbury proceeds. I got into town on Friday morning, and can prove that. I intended working his safe either Saturday or Sunday night. I have a passage booked for Canada, and if no one interferes, I shall sail from Liverpool on Thursday."

"Passport," said Knollis, holding out his hand.

Davidson sighed and handed it over. "Where were you on Thursday evening?"

"I dined at Stephano's, held an all-night party at my flat in Kingston Row, and left by car at eight-thirty in the morning."

"Proof?"

Davidson bowed elegantly from the waist. "I gave a lift to Brother Ignatius. I found him walking the wide road, the long road, the winding road made by the rolling English drunkard—Chesterton!—just outside Hatfield. I took him straight to the pub at Locksley, where he has been lying low and sayin' nuffin' ever since. Did you ever hear of such a perfect alibi, Inspector?"

"No better than a dozen others you've produced in the past five years," said Knollis. "Now get out, and stay in town! We might need you again."

Davidson sauntered to the door, cannoning into Burnell's plump waistline as he returned from the telephone.

"Letting you out?" demanded Burnell. "It's more than you deserve—but I shall catch up with you!"

Davidson politely held the door open for him, bowed him through, and then left them.

"Now, Mrs. Shardlow," said Knollis; "what can you tell us?"

"You seem to know most of it," she said quietly. "After Arthur went to prison I made up my mind to do something about it. I knew from his notes where to find some of the gang, so I transformed my appearance and went up to London for some days. I managed to make friends with Davidson, who obviously thought I was in the same line as himself, and he confided in me. He said he was in a tight spot with the Salisbury stuff, having given the Farthingale organisation the go-by. I suggested Cartland, and he fell for it. I then telephoned Cartland in Farthingale's name, and told him Davidson was coming up and the rest was left up to him."

Arthur Shardlow smiled across the room at his wife.

"You unprincipled woman!"

"I haven't finished being unprincipled," she said mysteriously. "Anyway, darling, he was a crook and deserved to go to prison! I only hoped they wouldn't be able to send him down for actually stealing them because he would have been out of circulation too long for my purposes. I sent him a note when he got out, and he came to Burnham to see me—"

"Excuse me," said Knollis, "but how did you manage to get the job with Cartland? That interests me tremendously!"

"Sorry, Inspector!"

"Oh, well, I'll have to find out for myself! Please carry on with your story."

"We fixed up a plan. Davy swore on oath he was finished with the game, but he wanted to fix the whole gang before he left the country—when he'd have to leave it, anyway! We decided to work through Cartland. I had seen mysterious parcels come by carrier and be taken away by Cartland, so I waited my chance, and when one came when he was at a Thursday luncheon, I persuaded the carrier to deliver it to Mr. Morley's shop."

She paused for a moment, and said in an innocent voice: "I can only guess the rest, of course."

"Of course!" her husband said dryly.

"Suppose you attempt to explain what might have happened?" Knollis suggested sarcastically.

"Well, I *think* Mr. Morley would open it without looking at the label. That's what I hoped would happen, at all events. He would find, I *think* stolen goods in it, and start to put two and two together. He's slow mentally, but even he should have managed that! He came to see Mr. Cartland after tea the same day, and they closed themselves in the office, and I *think* they were quarrelling because their voices were raised angrily several times. You see, we hoped Mr. Morley would expose him!"

She paused again, as if waiting for some comment, but no one said a word. Knollis sat with a peculiarly offensive smile on his thin lips, while the others gaped as if they were not quite sure they were hearing a story of double-crossing from this innocent-looking policeman's wife.

She continued: "You see, I had been in that upstairs room. Mr. Davidson had a key made from a wax mould I took when Mr. Cartland left his bunch in the office one day. We both had a look around one night . . ."

She smiled at Knollis. "You will forgive me for telling the untruth about never having been in the room before? You see, I didn't quite know how I stood then, and you didn't tell me a great deal, did you?"

Knollis got up and wiped his forehead with his handkerchief as he walked to the door. "Unprincipled, did you say, Mr. Shardlow? Heaven protect me from such a wife! She'll make you Assistant-Commissioner whether you want it or not!"

"Inspector!"

"Well, Mrs. Shardlow?"

"There are two women in the Vale who really *are* unprincipled!"

"Heaven help their consciences!" said Knollis.

CHAPTER VIII
PRIESTLY ADVICE

BROTHER IGNATIUS walked into Knollis's office absently, without knocking. He found Knollis apparently tied in a knot in his chair. He was in fact hugging his knees, and resting his chin on them while he tried to think his way through this most peculiar Cartland case. He blinked, shook himself, and jumped to his feet.

"Ignatius! I was coming to see you this afternoon."

"I anticipated your visit," smiled the little priest. "I may understand that you have arrived at the point where you now suspect Mr. Morley? When you have cleared him you will inevitably turn to Mrs. Morley."

"Leave your clairvoyant tricks out of it for the time being," said Knollis, somewhat irritably. "I want to ask you several questions. Firstly, did you travel to Burnham with Gentleman Davidson on Friday morning?"

"That is correct, Gordon," the priest nodded gravely. "He caught me up outside Hatfield when I was walking back to London."

Knollis stared at him bleakly. Walking *back* to London? Then Davidson was travelling toward town!"

The little priest smiled patiently. "Naturally, my dear Gordon. You didn't think he was driving in reverse, did you?"

"I'll do him!" exclaimed Knollis. Then he pause. "But you said you travelled to Burnham with him!"

"Yes, that is also correct. He gave me the news about Cartland's death, and said he was going to Burnham when he'd collected his luggage from the guest house at Hatfield in which he was staying. I went with him, and waited while he packed. Then we came on to Burnham together. He took me to the Ram and Crook Inn at Locksley, and he went to his lodging in town."

"Where had he been before returning to Hatfield?"

"Burnham."

"And where had *you* been if you were walking toward London?"

"Burnham." The little priest again said.

"Now, listen," said Knollis, putting one foot up on a chair and leaning on his knee. "How the devil—pardon the use of his name—had you got from Burnham to Hatfield by that time in the morning?"

Brother Ignatius continued to smile in a complacent manner that was rapidly infuriating Knollis.

"I flew it," he said. "So far as the devil is concerned, please don't hesitate to use his name, because I am intimately acquainted with him, and indeed would be very differently employed but for his existence. Yes, I flew with a Mr. Farthingale, who put me down in a meadow north of Hatfield, and then continued his journey to Sussex."

"Farthingale!" exclaimed Knollis.

He took a turn round the room and swung back to meet the little priest, his fingers tightly interlocked.

"Listen, Ignatius! Burnell has been on the blower to the Yard to fix up the arrest of Farthingale and about a dozen others. What do you know about him?"

"Who? Superintendent Burnell?"

"Farthingale!"

"We live in the same village. So did the Shardlows!"

Knollis stared down at the calm little man, and slowly unlocked his fingers and stretched them. "Why did you call here, Ignatius?"

"To assure you that the Morleys are both innocent of Roger Cartland's death."

"Ignatius," said Knollis," will you please do something for me? Will you please foam at the mouth, utter wild statements about what should be done to Cartland's murderer—or even get up and throw that vase of flowers at the wall? Anything but sit there looking smug! You know more about this case than the whole of the police force and the C.I.D. know, and you sit smugly playing with me!"

"I'm not smug, Gordon. I'm merely calm."

"You're not here to help me!"

"No," Brother Ignatius said calmly. "I don't believe in capital punishment. Neither do you. But whereas you only preach the doctrine, I try to practice the precept. I'm here solely to protect the innocent. *Vengeance is Mine, saith the Lord. I will repay.* Isn't that the law?"

"How long have we been friends?" asked Knollis with a note of dangerous calm in his voice.

Ignatius tapped his teeth with his knuckles. "Err—four years last Lady Day. Why?"

"Because in two minutes I'm going to ruin our friendship by shaking you to pieces! You wouldn't help me even if you knew the murderer! You do know him, too! Don't you?"

"I do know the name of the murderer," said Brother Ignatius slowly, "and I will not reveal his name, Gordon. Not unless there is a distinct possibility of an innocent person hanging in his stead. I merely called to tell you that neither of the Morleys could have been responsible for Cartland's death. I hoped you would accept my unqualified word for that, and turn your attention to other quarters."

"Why couldn't the Morleys have been responsible?"

"I cannot tell you that, Gordon. You may be able to persuade Joe Morley to tell you his story."

"He's told you something under seal of confessional?"

"Not that, but certainly something in confidence—which is just as sacred to me."

"And you know the murderer," Knollis said heavily.

"And why he murdered Cartland," added the priest. "It was my business to discover his identity."

"Ignatius, you are the most exasperating person I've ever known! It's also my business to discover Cartland's murderer—but do I get any help? Not on your blessed life!"

He glanced slyly at the priest, and said: "I'm bringing Morley in for questioning—and perhaps for more. He had a good motive, and he had an opportunity for putting aconite in the form of monkshood root into Cartland's grub. He has no alibi," he added thoughtfully.

Brother Ignatius stood up and smoothed his cassock with calm and unhurried hands. "I am not rising to the bait, Gordon. A little grilling with not hurt Morley, and knowing your stubborn nature I know you will have to prove his innocence to your own satisfactions—even while your intuition tells you he could not have been responsible for Cartland's death."

"Somebody pushed him down the hillside!"

Brother Ignatius did not answer.

"Davidson?" murmured Knollis. "Farthingale?"

"Goodbye, Gordon," said the priest.

Knollis went straight to the telephone and asked for Davidson to be fetched in again. "And he can stay a few hours this time," he said. "Nobody bluffs me more than once!"

He went into Manson's office to await Davidson's arrival, and while waiting sent a message to be delivered to Burnell as soon as he reported at the Yard, informing him of Farthingale's presence in Burnham on the Thursday night."

"I thought we'd cleared the deck to some extent by roping in the Farthingale mob," he said to Manson, "But we seem to be getting deeper in the mire."

"Horribly mixed metaphors," said Manson with a mock shudder.

Knollis ignored him. "Ignatius was in town that night, and so was Farthingale, and so was Davidson, and so was Morley. Interesting, ain't it?"

Manson scrawled lazily on the back of an envelope. "If Farthingale was in town it rather tends to solve the problem of what Cartland did between leaving Morley at the shop and dying in Locksley Vale. Yes?" he asked, looking up cautiously.

Knollis nodded sharply. "It could be the answer."

"It's seven miles from his shop to the Vale, and the airport forms a triangle with those two—you know what I mean! Here's Cartland's shop on Pilgrim Corner. The airport is here, four miles to the east of the city. Here's Locksley, seven miles to the north-east. Seems to me he could have met Farthingale, at the airport, and then gone home, either forgetting or ignoring the fact that Morley was waiting at Mayflower Street."

Knollis lit a cigarette and blew the smoke down his thin nostrils. "Cartland would be too ill to think about Morley."

"Which brings Farthingale in as the poisoner."

"No," said Knollis, shaking his head violently. "That is the snag the whole way through. The poison had got beyond his tummy. What I want to know just now is where Farthingale spend the night—because, according to Ignatius, he flew home early the next morning."

"The airport hotel, of course."

"There is one now?" asked Knollis. "In my days it was little more than a small flying field with the Burnham club's clubhouse attached."

"You wouldn't recognize it now," replied Manson. "It's the city's official airport."

He gave vent to a sudden oath. "I see now how Cartland got on to that ridge road! Coming from the airport he went straight on when he got to the cross-roads, so all that stuff about the camber taking his wheels round the bend means absolutely nothing!"

Knollis nodded absently.

"The C.C. will wig the ears off me," went on Manson. "I got you here for the right job, but for the wrong reason. Cartland wasn't necessarily driven through the gap by anyone! Don't you see it, Knollis? He came over the cross-roads instead of turning right, and then mistook the gap for the road leading down into the Vale! In other words, he missed the turn, and . . ."

Knollis gave a wry grin. "Ironic, isn't it? Yet if you hadn't made that mistake Cartland's death might have gone into the book as suicide. Yes, I'm inclined to agree with you, Manson."

"And this alters the complexion of the whole case!" Manson mumbled into the stem of his empty pipe. "By concentrating on the Shardlow angle you've unconsciously, opened up another line of investigation."

Knollis clicked his tongue. "That little Ignatius is correct, you know! You can use all the intelligence that the good God has given you, and then find there's something else inside you that works when you're asleep—whether your eyes are open or closed."

He turned as a sergeant ushered Gentleman Davidson into the room, still as dapper as ever, but looking somewhat apprehensive and suspicious this time.

"Send a shorthand writer," said Manson.

Knollis slid down in his chair, his leg extended. He made a temple of his fingers, with his cigarette held close to his lips. "You'd better find a comfortable pew, Davidson, because you look like being here a long time. You don't go until we're satisfied with your story this time. You don't put that one over me twice!"

Davidson gave a supercilious smile, prodded the nearest chair doubtfully, hitched his trousers, and gently lowered himself into it. "Mind if I smoke?"

"Not if you've anything to smoke," said Manson. "We might spring to a cup of tea when you're getting too hoarse to talk, but we don't run to salmon, cucumber, and cigarettes. Use that blinking ash-tray, too. This isn't a transport caff!"

"I happen to be a gentleman, Super."

"There's only your word for it!" Manson said curtly.

A girl walked in with a notebook and three pencils and went to a small table in the corner of the room.

"You can shoot now," said Manson.

"Where were you on Thursday night?" asked Knollis.

"In Burnham."

"Oh! So you admit it now!"

"Brother Ignatius has been to see you."

"Why did you tell the other story?"

"I thought you had me lined up for Cartland's job—and one doesn't always tell the truth in such circumstances. I was playing safe, and testing the ice I was walking on. Brother Ignatius tells me I've nothing to worry about if I tell the truth, so you shall have it."

"Thanks for the condescension," Knollis said sarcastically. "Don't over-strain your charity."

"Cut the cackle and get to the hosses, Davidson!" snorted Manson. "This isn't a *conversazione* in a suburban drawing-room, but a murder investigation."

"Yes, let's get working," said Knollis. "Why were you in town?"

"I told you I wanted to fix Cartland, and square the account. I've made enquiries, and learned that he attended his Thursday luncheon religiously, and regarded the rest of the day as a second half-holiday in the week, seldom going near the shop except to make sure his girl secured the doors properly."

"You got that from Mrs. Shardlow?"

"I didn't know who she was then," Davidson said glumly. "Never trust a woman, Inspector They've no principles—as we understand 'em!"

"That isn't bad, coming from you," said Knollis. "Having discovered those facts, what next?"

"I made it the night for breaking Cartland's safe."

"But you didn't?"

Davidson shook his head. "Not me! Somebody else was on the premises."

"Sure of that?" Knollis asked quickly. "Any idea—?"

"No," Davison replied, "but Brother Ignatius has asked me to clear Mr. Morley."

"How can you?"

"I went along to his place, and saw him moving about in the stock-room behind the shop. Stock-room, or office."

"At what time was this?"

"A quarter to nine—by the chimes of St. Giles's. I think it was a woman in Cartland's shop. The yard behind the shop is small, and enclosed by a brick wall about ten feet high. There was a whiff of scent hanging around, and a burning cigarette end on the blue-brick path—one with lipstick on it."

He put his hand inside his jacket and threw a stub on the table. "That's it."

Knollis glanced curiously at him. "Why did you bother to pick it up?"

"Mrs. Shardlow knew I was going in that night. She said she was going to the theatre. I wondered if she was double-crossing me in some way, and picked that up so that I could check on the brand she smoked."

"It belonged to her?"

"No. She smoked tipped cigs, and that one isn't—as even a detective can see."

"Shut up," snapped Knollis. "We don't need your sarcasm."

"The lipstick is the wrong shade, too," said Davidson. "Mrs. Shardlow has rotten taste—obviously not accustomed to daubing herself up in disguises—and uses orange-shaded stuff. That's on the crimson side, as you'll see. So it wasn't hers."

"Cars?"

"Not in the service lane, anyway. Neither was there any car parked in St. Giles's Lane. Neither was there one parked before the shop. All that checking was routine for me."

"What did you do?"

"Sheered off. I can speak plainly?"

"We'd like it," said Knollis.

"I've only kept out of your hands up to now by being careful. I like to see a few parked cars round a job—they're cheaper than taxis if a quick get-away is called for. No, I could see I wasn't wanted, so I cleared off."

"Lights in the premises?"

"Blinds down on the ground floor, but a chink of light showing down the edges of 'em."

"Did you go back later?"

Davidson shook his head. "I never work late. I like to get away while there are people on the streets—you're not so likely to be noticed then. I don't mind telling you all this now I've retired."

"Retired?" muttered Manson. "I'd hate to leave the Crown Jewels on the desk!"

"I'm a sensible man," said Davidson with a light bow. "I wouldn't be able to flog the Crown Jewels."

"What did you do next?"

Davidson pressed his cigarette in the tray with a knowing smile at Manson. "I went for a drink. I stayed at Pirelli's Club in Grove Street until one o'clock. Then I heard of Cartland's death, and times being as they were I decided it would be wise to establish an alibi as quickly as possible. I wasn't known at the club in my own name, so I was safe there. I motored through the night to Hatfield, where a room was permanently engaged. I drew in twice at transport caffs—your pronunciation, Super!—and spent about half an hour in each one, imbibing strong coffee to keep me awake and normally intelligent—"

"You should have tried a surgical operation," interrupted Manson.

Davidson coughed. "You must excuse the delays, Inspector Knollis. There's no co-operation. Anyway, I was running into Hatfield a few minutes before seven o'clock when I caught up with Brother Ignatius. I took him to the guest house—and left him outside in the car. I went in, chucked the maid under the chin, and told her I'd been for an early morning run, and had taken a cup of tea and a slice of toast while out. I went to my room, disturbed the bed, lathered my shaving brush and left it on the wash-bowl after daubing my razor with it. I let the towel fall in the water, and hung it over the rail to drip on the floor. I cut a cigarette in four pieces, lit them all, snubbed them out in the ash-tray—Superintendent Manson—and then went down and ran Brother Ignatius to Burnham."

"Fair enough," said Knollis. "We can check all that. Now what do you know about William Farthingale?"

Davidson shrugged, and sought another cigarette. "You know as much as I do."

"Any idea why Brother Ignatius was making for Hatfield? He obviously wasn't going home, or he could have been dropped much nearer."

"He was looking for me!" Davidson said grimly. "On hearing of Cartland's death he immediately wondered where I was. He couldn't find me in Burnham, so he went to the airport at dawn to see if he could hitch a lift down south. Farthingale was there—I wonder if he knew that—and Ignatius got his ride. Considering all things, I told him the whole truth, knowing *he* was capable of thinking it out."

"Thanks!" said Knollis.

"I took him to the inn at Locksley, and left him there, promising to be a good boy and stay at my digs in town until he gave the signal for me to clear out."

"Could you assume that Brother Ignatius had something to do with your conversion?"

Davidson grinned. "It hasn't been a conversion so much as a matter of learning and understanding economics. Brother Ignatius doesn't *preach*! He asked me for details of my—er—earnings over a five-year period, and proved beyond all doubt that there was more money to be made by applying my talents in other directions. He found me a job with a big lock and safe firm in Ontario!"

"Heaven help them!" exploded Manson. "In another five years you'll be capable of tackling the Bank of Canada!"

Davidson ignored the remark. "After all, they're the only things I really understand, and I think that if I'm given facilities for experiment I can eventually turn out a reasonably crack-proof safe."

"There isn't such a thing!" said Manson.

"I know that!" said Davidson. "All a safe-maker sells is time. He merely tries to make it more difficult for us—for cracksmen to crack. No, if the firm is a good one I should be quite happy with them."

"You'll have to postpone your sailing, you know," said Knollis. "We haven't finished with you yet."

"Oh, be damned!" said Davidson. "Don't I get a break now I am going straight?"

"I'll tell you what I'll do," said Knollis reflectively; "and heaven help you if you let me down! If Brother Ignatius will vouch for you I'll have a cable sent to Ontario saying you are temporarily helping the Yard, and we'll release you as soon as we can. That should add a certain cachet to Ignatius's testimonial. But if you do let me down you go in with Farthingale and Company!"

"That's near enough to condoning an offence," grumbled Manson.

"It's a white man's offer," said Davidson, "and I'll play ball with you."

He turned to the shorthand writer. "All right for pencils and freedom from writer's cramp? Then we'll proceed. Farthingale was the leader of the bunch—"

Manson intervened. "I can't let Knollis get away with all the decency, so I'll warn you! You realize you're turning Queen's Evidence? That what you say is useless unless it can be corroborated from other sources? And that we can give no promise that you will not be proceeded against on your own evidence!"

"In that case I'll keep my big mouth shut," said Davidson. "You're a queer pair of coppers—playing fair like this!"

Knollis tapped his knee impatiently. "So, there was a person, suspected to be a woman, in Cartland's premises at a quarter to nine on Thursday night, the night of Cartland's death? You found this cigarette stub still burning, in the yard. There was a trace of scent in the yard? All that is correct?"

"I'm prepared to sign my name to it!"

"You'll have to when it's been typed out. Don't worry about that," said Manson.

"Have you been near the premises since that time?"

"Not on your life, Inspector Knollis! Not after the owner gets himself murdered. Not Mr. Davidson!"

Knollis rose and stretched himself. "Thanks for everything, Davidson. You can wait in the outer office until the statement is ready for signing—and you shall have a cupper and a cigarette. You'll stay in town, of course, until we give you the word. Right?"

Davidson rose and stretched himself. He planted his hands on his slim hips and balanced himself on his toes. Then he sank back on his heels and looked cautiously at the two detectives.

"Can I give you a tip about the Shardlow case? It won't involve me at all, because I never saw it done, but I heard about it being done. You see, despite the fact that Mrs. Shardlow ditched me good and proper I still like the wench. She's got guts."

"What have you to tell us?" asked Manson.

"There's a method used in the States," Davidson said slowly, "and I don't think you people have got round to it yet. There's a method whereby dabs can be lifted from any smooth surface and replaced on another, or indeed taken away for laboratory purposes. The F.B.I and the police laboratories are using it regularly. I'm thinking about the dabs on the safe Shardlow is supposed to have opened—and he couldn't open a tin of sardines without a blowtorch and thermite! I have an idea they were grafted on from latent prints. Those footprints in the borders. A pair of his shoes were begged a week beforehand from his wife, and afterwards put in his dustbin an hour before Shardlow was taken up on the job."

"Thanks," said Knollis.

Davidson grinned nervously and fingered his carnation. "Funny, me helping the dicks! Here's something else that might help you. I collected this for my own protection, just like the fag-end."

He handed a sealed envelope to Knollis.

"Whoever went into Cartland's place that night went in like the thief in the Bible—by the back gate. She caught her suit on a nail that was sticking out of the gate-post. Those threads in there are what she left behind."

"Why did you do all this sleuthing?" Knollis asked cautiously.

"I've always made it a rule not to be taken for a job I haven't done—or for one that I have done, for that matter. My eyes have thrice saved me going down to the Moor for a holiday, Inspector. I could have gone down for a long spell for the Salisbury job—which I didn't do. I wanted the Salisbury stuff, but the Boss picked another bloke. He did it. I coshed him and relieved him of the proceeds, and then made one mistake—trying to flog 'em to Cartland. So I looked round when I saw somebody else in the place. *If* it was robbed, then *I* was in town, with no alibi. See what I mean?"

"Grey tweed, eh?" murmured Knollis as he opened the envelope. "I suppose these threads gave you ideas, eh, Davidson."

Davidson took out a very expensive cigarette case and offered it around. "No? Pity. These are extra specials from under the very best counters. Gave me an idea, you say? Like Brother Ignatius, I'm here for one reason only," he said with an impudent grin. "I'm here to protect the innocent—that's me!"

"You're about as innocent as Crippen!" said Manson.

CHAPTER IX
THE INNOCENT LADY

GORDON KNOLLIS was getting impatient with the Cartland case. He disliked physical clues, and up to now he had been held up from time to time while fingerprints, tin boxes, monkshood chippings, and pills had been laboratorised, as he scathingly called the work of the scientific department. The success of any case, in his own opinion, was dependent on a sound knowledge of human nature and its possibilities. Cartland had died a violent death. Ergo, someone had wanted him out of the way. That someone had to be capable of committing a murder. That someone needed a suitable opportunity. The solution of the case should depend on an intensive investigation into Cartland's connections, and a period of calm reflection on what his more learned colleagues called 'the psychology of the suspects.' And now he was held up again while the scientific wallahs went to work on the few shreds of grey tweed handed to him by Davidson. It was a lot of nonsense, as he told Manson in no uncertain terms.

"Patience!" said Manson. "Patience is what you need, my friend. Nobody ever got anywhere by rushing about like a blue-seated fly."

He sat back comfortably to await the report.

Knollis snorted, grabbed his hat from the peg, and walked out to the car parked in the courtyard behind the building. He drove out to the city airport, and there made enquiries about the arrival and departure of William Farthingale. He learned that he had arrived at four o'clock on the Thursday afternoon, had taken tea in the airport hotel, booked a room there for the night, entertained a lady at dinner, sent her away in a taxi, had stayed the night and left early the next morning—and if he wanted to know the exact minute he would have to consult the Traffic Controller.

Knollis was not too interested in the time of Farthingale's departure, but he was very interested in the lady who had been dined, and, presumably wined. It shouldn't have been Mrs. Shardlow, because she was at the theatre—or was she?

He went to the restaurant and found the waiter who had attended Mr. Farthingale's table. Yes, the lady was with him, a middle-aged lady in good condition, well-spruced up and all that, sir. They seemed to be talking confidential matters because they stopped talking every time he approached the table. They sat down about ten minutes after seven, and the lady left at somewhere around ten to a quarter past eight. He ordered the taxi at the gent's request, and the address given was the Embassy Club, and the taxi was owned by Charles Tollerton who lived at No. 84 Maddison Avenue, Burnham.

Knollis went to Maddison Avenue. Mr. Tollerton produced the driver who had brought the fare from the airport. No, he didn't know her name, although he thought the gent might have called her Mrs. Vale when he put her in the taxi. She was a well-built woman of something over fifty, but nowhere near sixty, a buxom woman wearing some sort of fur coat, and he didn't know the difference between skunk, rabbit, and silver fox—if there was any difference at all. It was dark-coloured, and that was all he could say. He left her outside the club, and she tipped him two shillings—why, thank you, Sir! She was seen off from the airport by a merry, chubby little man who was smoking a good cigar, judging by the air around him. He might not know fur coats, but he did know a good cigar when he got the chance to try one. He dropped the lady at half-past eight.

Knollis looked at his watch. It was half-past five. He drove to the Vale of Locksley to see Gabby Jones. She smirked happily at him probably remembering the half-crown he had given her.

"Gabby," he said, "Can you remember what time it was when Mrs. Cartland left for Wainfleet?"

"Ha'past eight. Mes' Cartland left same time."

"Does Mrs. Morley often call?" he asked casually. "Mrs. Cartland and Mrs. Morley are good friends?"

And then he learned something from the girl's ramblings that interested him. About a fortnight before the murder Mrs. Morley had called on Mrs. Cartland. They had shut themselves in the drawing-room, and there had been what Manson would have termed a first-class bull-and-cow. A row. When Gabby took coffee in half an hour later she found Mrs. Cartland in tears, and Mrs. Morley looking "indi'nant and mad-like." Mrs. Morley stayed another twenty minutes, and then showed herself out, marching down the drive "wive her 'ead all up 'i the air like."

Knollis now dearly wanted a chat with Mrs. Shardlow, but did not want Mrs. Cartland to get suspicious, so he called at the house with a lame story about passing that way and wondering if by any chance Miss Shawbrook needed a lift into town. He sat twiddling his fingers for ten minutes while she just slipped something on, and then escorted her to the car.

Once on the road he started asking questions.

"Are you with us, or against us, Mrs. Shardlow?"

She gave him a look of intense surprise. "With you, of course—if only for Arthur's sake, but at the same time I want to put Mrs. Cartland straight so that she can run the business."

"Suppose Mrs. Cartland should prove to be implicated—even as an accessory after the fact?"

"That would necessarily alter my attitude. Is she?"

"I don't know," said Knollis, "and that is an honest-to-God straight answer. You may be able to help me. Do you happen to know whether she has a suit or costume at the cleaners—or the invisible menders?"

"Why yes! She sent her grey tweed jacket. She snagged it on a rose bush while pruning."

"Can you get the name and address of her sister at Wainfleet?"

"I've got it, having posted a letter for her. Florence Horton, Bolingbroke Drive."

"Thanks," Knollis said laconically. "Is Mrs. Morley still paying social or duty calls at the house?"

"Mm, she is," Mrs. Shardlow said slowly. "She and Mrs. Cartland have held several private sessions over something or other."

Knollis was silent until he showed Mrs. Shardlow into her husband's room. "I'll call for you in an hour's time," he said. "Please be ready."

He went on to headquarters and put through a call to the Wainfleet police.

"A Mrs. Florence Horton lives at Bolingbroke Drive. She's the sister of our Mrs. Cartland . . . yes. Mrs. Cartland is supposed to have motored there on Thursday last. Can you check time of arrival for me? Thanks."

He stooged round for fifty minutes until the reply came. Mrs. Cartland had arrived shortly before midnight, having been delayed by a puncture and plug trouble. A heavy-transport driver had changed the wheel for her.

"Very nice," said Knollis. "Thanks again."

He picked up Mrs. Shardlow and drove her back to Locksley Vale, where he asked for a private interview with Mrs. Cartland.

"At what time did you arrive at Wainfleet on Thursday?" he asked.

Mrs. Cartland buffed her right hand fingers in her left palm. "Oh, sixish."

Knollis raised his eyebrows. "Any advance on six?"

Mrs. Cartland saw the red light. "We-ell, it was a little later, actually. You see, I had tyre trouble on the way."

"Probably due to eating too good a dinner," said Knollis gravely. "Have you a grey costume with a tear on the right sleeve?"

"Why yes! I tore it on a rose in the garden. Why?"

"Some shreds of grey tweed were found on a nail in a gate-post at the rear of your Pilgrim Corner shop, Mrs. Cartland."

She said "Oh!"

"We have a description of a buxom woman wearing a grey costume who was on those premises at a quarter to nine. What brand of cigarettes do you smoke, Mrs. Cartland?"

"Er—why, Rosswell's Goldflake, Inspector."

"The stub of a Rosswell's Goldflake was found in the yard—still burning. There was lipstick on it—the same shade as that you are now wearing. I'll take a guess at Pershore's No. 3."

Mrs. Cartland strode with mannish strides to the window, and said: "Oh, my Gord!"

Knollis waited silently.

"It looks bad, doesn't it?" she ventured.

"Curious, at least."

"I'd a good reason for being there!"

"When your husband thought you were at Wainfleet? You arrived there at midnight, so you must have driven like the devil himself. It must have been a most urgent call you paid at the shop!"

"I had to go there, Inspector. I—I suspected my husband and—Miss Shawbrook!"

"Come off it," Knollis said, descending to the vernacular. "You were looking for something."

"Yes. Yes, of course."

"You found it?"

"Yes."

"It satisfied you—or did it merely shake you?"

She turned and looked at him, slowly and at length. "You know, don't you?"

"I know," said Knollis.

"It knocked the bottom clean out of my world. I can't remember driving to Wainfleet. I was driving there to get away from Burnham and Locksley, and I did not intend to return."

"Who told you?"

"I want to forget that, too!"

"Mrs. Morley?"

She lowered her head.

"And now?" asked Knollis. "What do you propose now?"

"I honestly don't know, Inspector. I don't know what proportion of our money was made honestly. That's why I have Miss Shawbrook with me. I'm trying to assess the amount I can honestly use for my own purposes. She's helping me enormously—although she doesn't know the truth, naturally!"

"Naturally," agreed Knollis. "And the rest of the money? What will you do with that?"

"Well, unless you can prove where it came from so that it can be returned, I shall give it to various charities, anonymously."

"Who killed your husband, Mrs. Cartland?"

She walked to the table and pressed her knuckles hard down the edge of it. Her lips tightened, and her eyes narrowed.

"Kathleen Morley!"

Knollis was not surprised by the accusation, but he could not leave it there as a statement unqualified.

"Mrs. Morley, eh?" he murmured softly. "Now why should you suggest Mrs. Morley?"

"She came to me a short while ago—a fortnight before Roger's death, and told me he was a criminal. She said all the proof was at Pilgrim Corner. She said Roger had made a fool, a monkey, and an unsuspecting criminal of her own innocent and honest husband. Roger, she said, was trying to persuade Joe to join him as a willing partner in crime. She said Joe couldn't very well expose Roger without exposing himself as *the* most unworldly innocent, or without people thinking he wasn't innocent and was trying to expose Roger to save himself. She put forward a most complicated series of explanations, and finally said the men apparently couldn't find a solution, and we two women had to do something."

"All this at one interview?" Knollis asked in a doubtful voice.

Mrs. Cartland shrugged. She took a cigarette from the box on the table, and pushed it across to Knollis. He held his lighter for her, and she puffed the cigarette into life.

"She's hardly been off the doorstep since. I had to prove her story one way or another, and Thursday was my first chance. I knew Roger was going to the usual luncheon, and I knew he had some business in the evening. I ascertained it was not to be conducted at the shop. I made arrangements to go to Wainfleet for one good reason. If I proved Kathleen Morley to be correct I wanted to be well away from Roger while I thought out what to do—and I knew I couldn't dissemble sufficiently well to deceive him; he would be bound to realise something was wrong. I spent most of the day in Newark with an old friend, and returned to Burnham to look around the shop. A spare key to the rear door was kept at home, and I managed to have duplicates made of Roger's keys. He 'lost' them for a day, and later found them in the greenhouse."

Knollis smiled inwardly. This was the second bunch of duplicates that had been made. He wondered what Cartland would have said if ever he had found out.

Marion Cartland looked at Knollis for a moment, and then said: "I saw everything needful, Inspector. I knew you would ask me about it sooner or later, since it was bound to be discovered after Roger's death in such circumstances."

"You think Mrs. Morley was responsible! Why, Mrs. Cartland?"

She was some moments in answering. "I think she knew before he husband did that everything was not right at the shop. You will have heard about the somewhat frank talk on criminology given to us by Sir Edmund Griffin? She later asked a question. She said Sir Edmund had suggested it was possible to commit murder in such manner that the culprit was never suspected. Would he, she asked, be prepared to qualify the statement?"

"And then?"

"Sir Edmund was loth to reply, and said that if he answered it would be on the understanding that he would not be pressed with supplementary questions, since the subject was one for discussion in police circles."

"His reply to the question?" asked Knollis, as if he knew nothing about the talk.

"He said the resulting death should appear to be the result of an accident, suicide, or natural death," Mrs. Cartland quoted significantly.

"Quite a comprehensive answer!" said Knollis.

"I chided her. I told her she should never have asked such an embarrassing question. She giggled, and said you never knew when the information might come in useful!"

"She said that?" murmured Knollis. "And you think . . ."

"Quite candidly, Inspector, I believe she poisoned Roger, considering that the only solution to our problem."

"How?" Knollis asked laconically.

"My maid, as you know, is part-witted. She tells me she found Mrs. Morley prowling round the garden during the course of Thursday afternoon. Gabby left a cold-meat tea for Roger—Roger was always fond of heavy meals in spite of his alleged gastric troubles. She left for him—"

"Cold beef and horseradish sauce," said Knollis.

Marion Cartland hesitated. "I have heard that it is possible to mistake the root of monkshood for horseradish."

"Where have you heard that?"

"Roger heard some talk on horticulture at a Rotary meeting. Is it correct?"

"*If* Mrs. Morley left monkshood root on the radish clamp my Gabby would pick the first roots she saw, take them to the kitchen, and make them into a sauce."

"But did she?"

Mrs. Cartland went as far as her gentility would allow to an indignant snort. "Gabby says she saw the radishes lying on the heap, and thought either my husband or myself had dug them out for her to use."

"You can rely on her statement?"

"She hasn't the intelligence to imagine or lie, Inspector. Gabby's world is a matter-of-fact and objective one. She sees, she describes, and that is as far as her brain will allow her to go."

Knollis wiped a hand across his forehead, and took a turn around the room. "There's something wrong, Mrs. Cartland. The poison that killed your husband was part-digested. It had passed from his stomach to his intestines. Pardon all these physical details, but you must know the facts if you're to help us. As an educated woman you understand the process of digestion. There were traces of aconite in your husband's stomach, but not enough to do more than make him ill. Certainly not enough to kill him."

"Does physical tolerance enter into the problem, Inspector?"

Knollis shook his head. "Dr. Robbins says not."

"Then *two* doses must have been administered!"

"That is a possibility," Knollis admitted.

Marion Cartland poised a thoughtful finger on her cheek. "He had cereal, bacon and egg, and toast and marmalade for breakfast—all of which I prepared and served myself. He took luncheon with the Thursday Society. He had tea at home, and seemingly dined with Joe Morley at the Spaniels—"

"On plaice and tartare sauce," interrupted Knollis.

He watched Marion Cartland slowly, saw comprehension creep into her mind and be expressed on her full features in horror.

"My God!" she said in a whisper.

Knollis took out a cigarette and lit it, and watched her over the top of his lighter, watched her with narrowed eyes. She turned to the fireside chair and slowly sank on the edge of it, staring bleakly at the carpet. Then her control deserted her. She buried her face in her hands and began to sob. Knollis walked to the window and watched a thrush pull a reluctant worm from the lawn. In some remote fashion there was a kinship between himself and the thrush. For the past half-hour he had been planning to draw a reluctant admission from the woman sobbing behind him.

He stood a long while, until he had smoked his cigarette and lit another from it, and stubbed out the old in the soil surrounding a potted plant on the table beside him.

"You—you knew the truth, Inspector!" Mrs. Cartland whispered.

"I suspected it, Mrs. Cartland."

"I have to face it! I can't refuse to deny the facts. It was Roger—it was Roger who was trying to—to poison Joe Morley!"

"I think so, Mrs. Cartland," said Knollis evenly. "I think he deliberately chose the meal because the monkshood would not be tasted beneath the natural sharp taste of the sauce. I think he took a small dose home so that both of them would be ill, but so that he would recover. I think he planted the roots on the radish clamp for Gabby to use. You know, the symptoms of aconite poisoning are very similar to those of food poisoning, and it is not always identified during analyses.

"We know he found an excuse to send Morley down to the telephone. Later he went down to the cloak-room, and Mrs. Wooderson found a typewriter ribbon box behind the radiator—containing chippings of monkshood root. Some new and apparently more powerful indigestion pills had arrived for him that afternoon, and we know he took one immediately before going up to the Crusader Room to dinner. We believe he had taken others previously. They would help him to overcome the effects of the tartare sauce he was going to eat with Morley, and the mild dose of aconite he had absorbed with his tea."

Mrs. Cartland stared at him. "But Joe was not ill at all!"

"That is one of the puzzling features of the case," said Knollis. "We can only assume that your husband made a mistake and sat down to the wrong plate. However, we shall work our way through that one, and in the meantime, we have another problem on our hands."

"And what will that be, Inspector?" Marion Cartland asked as she still dabbed her eyes.

"We can't understand why you met Mr. Farthingale at the airport."

"Oh! You know about that!"

"All of it," Knollis said calmly, "even to what you ate and drank, at what time you arrived, at what time you left, and the name of the taxi-driver who dropped you outside the Embassy Club at half-past eight."

"There's no reason why I shouldn't have met him," she replied indignantly. "William's my brother!"

Knollis stared stupidly at her, and exclaimed: "What? Your brother!"

"I needed advice from someone, Inspector!"

Knollis flicked the remains of his cigarette into the hearth and gave a silly and most uncertain laugh.

"What's funny about that, Inspector?" Marion Cartland demanded.

"Sorry," said Knollis. "My nerves seem to be going to pieces. So you asked advice of Mr. Farthingale. What *did* he advise, Mrs. Cartland?"

"He admitted the whole affair was shameful, and for that reason alone we must ensure that Roger was not exposed, or it would recoil on all of us. He said he would think the thing out most carefully, and find a way of convincing Roger that he must be content to earn his living as an honest man. He advised me to go to Wainfleet and leave everything to him."

Knollis felt like kicking something—hard. He restrained himself and instead asked a question. "Your home was at Lonsdale St. Peter's?"

"We're a long-established Lonsdale family."

"Then you know Brother Ignatius?"

"Very well indeed!"

"The village constable, Shardlow?"

She shook her head. "It's eleven years since we left the village, Inspector."

"Thank God for that!" muttered Knollis, thinking about Mrs. Shardlow sitting in the next room.

CHAPTER X
TEA FOR TWO

IF GORDON KNOLLIS had been a serious student of psychology he would have gravitated to the Gestalt school of thought, being a great believer in patterns. In spite of the doubts which had assailed him during past years, those he had hesitatingly expressed to Brother Ignatius in the restaurant so many months ago, he was still inclined to the belief that there were patterns in every human life, and that it was his task to discover them. He sought one in every case he investigated, and at no time more energetically than in the Cartland case.

The investigation of a murder was something like the putting together of a jigsaw puzzle. You found a piece of a certain shape and colour, and tried it first here, and then there, in the hope it would fit and match. Finding it did not, you put it aside for a time, and eventually found a space in which it would be at home. Then you were a stage nearer the completion of the puzzle, a stage nearer the minute when you would see the whole picture.

It was mainly a matter of infinite patience, and Knollis sometimes wished life was a wee bit more like the books, with exciting chases by car, motor-launch, and aircraft.

He spent an hour discussing the case with Manson over several glasses of Mr. Wooderson's excellent ale, and went to bed at a quarter to eleven. The lace factory opposite worked a night shift, and the weird blue-green light from the mercury-vapour lamps filtered into the room through the flowered curtains, accompanied by the soft and lulling hum of the machines. It was not unlike being in a seaside aquarium with a Wurlitzer organ playing in some remote alcove.

He lay awake for some time, trying to assemble the pieces of the Cartland puzzle, which he admitted to be as baffling as any he had encountered. Lonsdale St. Peter's was the background of the picture, and there was little doubt about that. Marion Cartland, William Farthingale, Brother Ignatius, and Arthur and Mrs. Shardlow all came from Lonsdale. In that peaceful Sussex village, with its white-railed village green and tree-lined roads, the first plan had been formed. From that evil inspiration had grown the jewel of a gang which had defied the best efforts of Scotland Yard and many provincial forces for all too long. From it had sprung other evils; the conviction of an innocent policeman, and the murder of Roger Cartland. From it, too, had come the disintegration of the gang. The scheme, from the outset, had carried within the seeds of its own decay.

The gang were now as good as in the bag. The evidence kept so foolishly in Cartland's secret records had provided sufficient excuse for the round-up which would now be in progress in London and the Home Counties.

The telephone bell on the bedside shrilled loudly, startling him. He sat bolt upright in the half-darkness swearing softly. He lifted the handset, to hear Wooderson speaking from his private exchange in the parlour.

"Sorry to disturb you, Inspector. The Yard are on the line. Superintendent Burnell wants you urgently."

"Put him through," said Knollis.

"Burnell here," said a faraway voice. "Bad news for us. Farthingale got away in that kite. I can only assume that he realised the game was up when Mrs. Cartland told him what she knew—"

"Oh well, we'll pick him up somewhere!" Knollis interrupted irritably.

"I don't think so," Burnell replied slowly. "A destroyer has reported seeing a light cabin plane going down into the sea. They went to the spot, but found only stray ends of wreckage drifting about. It was flying towards Holland, by the way. Sorry, old man!"

Knollis said goodnight, and replaced the handset. So that was that! But even with Farthingale safely in Davy Jones's Locker he had to make sure whether Cartland had or had not seen him at the airport. Mrs. Cartland dined with Farthingale at ten minutes past seven, so it could be assumed she arrived at seven. Had Cartland seen Farthingale before his wife's visit? Or was he with him afterwards? His wife left at a quarter past eight.

Cartland crashed at half-past nine. If he went to see Farthingale after his wife's visit . . .

He switched on the bedside lamp, reached for a notebook and pencil, which he always kept beside the bed. He made out what he always called a list of runners and riders, although he was no racing man.

Cartland's Movements

12:30 Arrival at Saracen's Head for the Thursday Society Luncheon. Talking in bar.

1:00 Luncheon

3:00 Left hotel, dropped Morley at Mayflower Street, and went home to Locksley.

? Left home.

6:20 Arrived at Spaniels.

7:00 Dinner with Morley.

8:15 Came down from Crusader Room.

8:30 Left Spaniels. Collected key from Mrs. Shardlow. Left Morley at Mayflower Street.

9:30 Crashed.

9:45 Died.

That was one man's day—his last one. Knollis grunted as he surveyed the evidence. If Cartland saw Farthingale before dining with Morley he did it between taking tea at home and his arrival at the Spaniels. If he saw him after leaving the Spaniels it must have been long after a quarter to nine. In either case he travelled two sides of the triangle within the hour. It didn't seem likely, on the face of it, that he had gone to the airport. If he saw Farthingale at all it surely must have been between Farthingale's arrival time—four o'clock—and his own arrival at the Spaniels at twenty minutes past six.

What a problem! He closed the notebook, switched off the light, and went to sleep. He slept badly, sharing his time between rescuing Farthingale's jewel-packed suitcase from the depths of the North Sea and twisting the arms of Brother Ignatius in the hope that he would tell what he knew.

After breakfast next morning he drove straight out to the airport and requested an interview with the manager of the restaurant. The latter found the waiters who had been on duty, but in spite of Knollis's best efforts he failed to prove that Farthingale had entertained anyone but Mrs. Cartland. The result was logical, and only what he could have expected, but he remained disappointed. It was obvious that the two men would not want to be seen together. What then, had Cartland done with himself after arriving home for tea?

He went back to police headquarters and asked Manson to send two or three men out to Locksley to seek news of Cartland's movements during the tea-hour. He filled in the time by writing-up his reports for the Chief Constable and the Yard.

The news shook him when it arrived. He was muttering to himself when Manson joined him in the office.

"Heard it?" he asked.

Manson nodded. "Met Mac on the way in. So Mrs. Morley entertained the late but not lamented Mr. Cartland to tea! Kept nicely quiet about it, hasn't she? But what happened to the meal the dim maid left for him?"

"God only knows," said Knollis. "This is some case! Mrs. Morley was seen going to his house at half-past three, and Cartland later took tea with her. At all events it proves that Cartland went straight home from Burnham."

"It could mean that Robins was wrong about the aconite," commented Manson. "It could also mean that Mrs. Cartland is correct in suspecting Kathleen Morley."

Knollis pulled the lobe of his ear. "There's a catch in this case somewhere, Manson. I'll find it if it takes me a year. Darned if I'll be beaten! Anyway, this means we have to interview her again. As things are, we'd better go straight away."

"Might be as well," Manson agreed. "If she learns we've been making enquiries in the village she might start thinking up a good story to account for her activities. Let's go."

Joe Morley opened the door to them. He looked them up and down, scowled, and held the door wide open for them to accept an unspoken invitation to step inside. He closed the door behind them, took their hats, and then asked: "What's it *this* time?"

"We really came to see your wife," Knollis said thoughtfully, "But it occurs to me we might make a family party of it. Your wife is available?"

Morley puts the hats on pegs, and gave a weary grimace.

"I'll see. Wait in here, will you?"

He showed them into the sitting-room and left them.

"Bloke's beginning to look a bit under the weather," said Manson. "Wonder if he's got anything on his mind?"

"Don't be facetious," said Knollis. "If he has we can remove it for him before we go. In any case you can't expect him to be looking joyful and triumphant. He doesn't know all we know, and he *was* the last person believed to have seen Cartland alive, and he did eat with him not long before his death."

"He could have done it," Manson said stubbornly. "I still haven't lost hope of getting him. Y'know, these murder cases make a nice change, but I wouldn't want one per month."

"This is my ninth major murder case," said Knollis. "I like the intellectual exercise, but the emotional strain tends to get me down. You absorb the moods of the other characters to some extent. You've the wife or husband of the deceased, and the wives and husbands of the suspects, all taut and strained, with some of them on the very edge of hysteria, and nervous witnesses getting worked up about their inevitable appearances in court. You've the lack of sleep, the long days, and the urgency of the investigation. All those things play hell with you. I'm often accused of being a poker-faced, unsociable, and unfeeling man, but the truth is that if I didn't keep a tight hold on myself I'd sometimes break into tears as a result of sheer nervous exhaustion. As it is, I'm like a squeezed-out sponge by the time I have a job all nicely tied up. Then, of course, I don't like the morning when the client is hanged . . ."

"They mostly deserve it," said Manson.

"Somebody said, in the sixteenth century—wasn't it Sir Henry Wotton?—that hanging was the worse use a man could be put to.

That is also my opinion. It's all wrong, and not in keeping with the religious opinions we, as a nation, pretend to observe—"

Morley entered the room, leading his wife by the hand. Both looked pale and serious. Morley looked as if nothing but his hands had combed his hair for several days. His wife was neatly dressed in a well-cut blue suit, but as she favoured an untidy hair-style it was impossible to tell whether she had dressed it or not, although her free hand told its tale as it twiddled nervously with a button.

Morley suggested they might all be seated. "It will make things look more homely, and less official," he said shakily. "It appeared probable to Knollis that Morley and his wife had engaged in a heart-to-heart talk while she was changing out of her house clothes, and that Joseph Pevensey had learned something he had not known before. He was extremely ill at ease.

"Why have you come?" he asked hesitatingly.

"We'd like to know why your wife entertained Cartland to tea last Thursday," said Knollis.

Morley made a pretense of being surprised. "He was *here*, Kath?" he said lamely.

She looked at the floor and nodded. "Ye-es, you see, I thought—"

"Before we go any further," said Knollis, "it might be as well to remove any misunderstandings. We know Cartland was a receiver on a large scale. We know he was in business with his brother-in-law, Farthingale—"

"Farthingale!" Morley exclaimed.

"You didn't know that, Mr. Morley? Farthingale was what the more sensational papers call the Master Mind."

"I knew," said Kathleen Morley. "Mrs. Cartland went to see him about Roger. She didn't know her brother was a crook—and I didn't feel like telling her!"

"We'll come back to that in a few minutes," said Knollis.

"We know your husband was aware of Cartland's activities. We know he has told you. We know you challenged Mrs. Cartland with the information. We know Davidson was a member of the gang and had decided to break away. We know he was shopped by Cartland. Now, Mrs. Morley, why did you entertain him to tea?"

"He didn't know his wife knew about him. I persuaded him to come to tea so that I could play it as the last card, as the trump card. Joe had failed to move him, and Marion couldn't find a solution, so I invited him to tea and threatened to tell her. He laughed at me, and that was where I told him she already knew, and was dying of shame . . ."

"Well?"

"It knocked all the stuffing out of him. I didn't think he was capable of it, but he started to blubber like a child, and I began to regret telling him. He said it really was the end. Marion was the only person who had ever had faith in him. He'd worked his way from the slums, and she'd married him despite knowing his beginnings. He didn't know what he was going to do now. If I hadn't been so sorry for Joe and myself I could have been sorry for him."

"What did you give him for tea?"

"My last tin of black-market salmon," she said wryly. "I made it into a salmon salad."

"With mayonnaise?"

"I made mayonnaise, but he would touch it because of his weak tummy. He said it was off, and he took two pills before tea."

"Ah!" said Knollis.

Kathleen Morley gave him a curious glance. "Is that significant, Inspector?"

"Tell me about them," Knollis replied.

"They were new ones that had arrived. He'd found them waiting for him when he got home. They were still wrapped, and I saw him unwrap them. There was a note from the firm enclosed. He explained that they were some new recipe, and they wanted him to try them."

"What happened to the note?"

"He—yes, he threw it in the fireplace."

"So it was burned?"

"No, it should be there yet. I had an electric fire burning—you know how the coal situation is!"

"Which room?"

"The dining-room."

"Excuse me," said Knollis. He went into the dining-room, few out the fire-screen, and fished among a good collection of empty cigarette packets and orange peel. Mrs. Morley apparently didn't object to untidiness providing it was hidden. He found the screwed-up note bearing the address of Grove & Meadows, herbalist, of Leicester. He put it in his wallet and returned to the dining-room.

"I found it," he said. "You say he took two of the pills?"

"Two, apologizing to me. He said it was not an oblique insult to my food, but he had such awful pains he had to take strict measures with himself."

"And that was before tea!"

"Yes."

"The time?"

"Oh, about quarter to four as near as I can say. Between then and four o'clock anyway."

"He took any afterwards?"

"Yes, with more apologies. He took one to counteract the vinegar in the salad. I, in turn, apologised for that."

"So you made him weep," said Knollis. "Did you reach any solution of the problem?"

Kathleen Morley shook her head. "No, but he said he was glad Marion was away. It would give him time to think before she came back. His actual words were: *I don't know how I shall face her, and I've got to have something to tell her!*"

"What did you say to that, Mrs. Morley?"

"I was regaining my confidence, and I suggested that if he were to throw up the whole game, and make restitutions as well as he could, it might never be mentioned between himself and his wife—I could fix that. A conspiracy of silence might be entered into by all concerned."

"That's condoning a felony," muttered Manson. "You would all be accessories after the fact."

Kathleen Morley gave him a twisted smile. "We were prepared to have that on our consciences, Super. There are times
when even the most rigid of consciences can sideslip the law
without feeling uneasy. My point was that if we could agree—if
Roger would agree to drop the game, we might persuade Marion
to pretend she knew nothing about it, and I'd admit I'd bluffed
him—while still threatening to tell her if he backed out. That
was the real trump card."

"What were you doing across at his place at half-past three?"

"Looking for him of course. He came up the drive while I
was there and I went in with him. He sorted his mail and put the
packages in his pocket. He said he'd be only too glad to have tea
with me because he hated an empty house."

"Wasn't there a meal laid out for him?"

"Yes. Something between two plates, and a boat of sauce.
There was also a plate of bread and butter with another plate
over it."

"There's always a boat of sauce," said Manson, "and Cartland
didn't take sauce!"

"How long had you held this idea of entertaining him?"

"Since noon."

"Did you mention the laid-out meal?"

"I said perhaps he wouldn't want to come as the meal was
ready but he grinned and said he'd cope with it later—perhaps
for supper."

"There was other mail apart from the package?"

"Two or three letters, Inspector. He left it on the table."

"There's a point!" exclaimed Manson.

"I've noticed it," said Knollis. He nudged Manson and they
left the house. There was a curious expression on Manson's sun-
burned features.

"Why didn't you tackle Morley?" he demanded. "I thought
you'd put that on the agenda?"

"You mean about the Spaniels meal? Getting desperate,
aren't you? How the deuce can I say more about it in the light
of Robins' report? Robins states that he took the fatal dose long
before he arrived at the inn, and What's-his-name, the patholo-

gist has confirmed it. There's nothing I can accuse him of so far as I can see."

"And where are we going now?"

"To see Gabby Jones, aren't we? I thought you said there was another point?"

Then Knollis said: "Oh, Lord!"

He led the way back to Morley's front door and rang the bell. "Sorry about this," he said when Kathleen Morley appeared, "but I forgot to ask one vital question. At what time did Cartland leave you?"

"Six o'clock. No, it would be a little earlier, because I remembered switching on the radio as he left and Children's Hour was still on. Perhaps ten to six."

"He went back to the house for the car?"

"Oh, no! We came across in his car. He drove towards Burnham, having to see Joe on some business. We agreed not to let my husband know he had been to tea."

"Thanks," said Knollis. Judging by his tone he might as well have said: "Thanks for nothing!"

At the Cartland house he asked a question of Gabby. "When you arrived here on Friday morning, did you see any of the afternoon mail lying around?"

She did not. The table was cleared, the plates and dishes washed, wiped, and put away, and the whole dining room was tidy.

"Tell Mrs. Cartland I'd like to see her," said Knollis.

While they were waiting for her Manson said: "That was what she told us in the first interview! What's on your mind now?"

"You'll see—or you won't," said Knollis.

Mrs. Cartland looked askance as Knollis asked his question. "Call back at the house? I assure you I didn't! You know what time I left Burnham, and you checked my time of arrival at Wainfleet. Who do you think I am, Inspector? Stirling Moss or Michael Hawthorne?"

"Why did you have the taxi run you back from Burnham?"

"Because a taxi took me there! I didn't want to run the risk of meeting Roger, because he would surely have recognised the car! And so of course I went back to town to pick it up."

"And you didn't call at the house?"

"I swear it, Inspector. Why?"

"Because if you didn't, then somebody else did!"

CHAPTER XI
REVISION BY DAVIDSON

MANSON LET IN the clutch and asked in which direction he should drive.

"Anywhere you like. Just dawdle round," replied Knollis. "I want to think. You want to think. We all want to think."

"Where is the pen of the aunt of my gardener?" murmured Manson.

"Why did Mrs. Morley go back to Cartland's house?"

"Did she?"

"Who else could have done so?" countered Knollis. "Morley was in town. Mrs. Cartland was with Farthingale. Cartland was with Morley—and we can assume that Morley was with Cartland."

"That's really good thinking, Knollis," said Manson. "Must have taken you some time to arrive at that conclusion!"

"I can't imagine Cartland going back to clear the tea-table. That kind of man believes women are only on earth to do domestic chores and minister to the Lord and Master of the Household. No, Mrs. Morley was right when she said she drove to Burnham."

"He could have slipped back to deal with the cold beef!"

"On top of salmon? In any case, the time factor supports her."

"He seems to have been something of a pig," said Manson, "so I was justified in wondering! By the way, what's your opinion of this eat-sauce, don't-eat-sauce angle?"

"Simply explained," said Knollis. "Cartland wanted attention and sympathy. Never met a bloke like that? Non-existent headaches and migraines? Dicky tummies? He was always drawing attention to himself, and foregoing of sauces, spices, pickles, and high seasonings while at home was one way of keeping the little woman attentive and sympathetic—although it seems she had rumbled him but was prepared to play his game."

"Yet Gabby prepared sauce for him!"

"Some daft people aren't daft in all respects, Manson. She probably knew he would lap it up as a cap laps cream if nobody was there to watch him. Yet as soon as he gets with Mrs. Morley he puts on the act again. For the point I was originally talking about, Mrs. Morley is the only one for it."

"Knollis," Manson said earnestly, "suppose the two Morleys planned to do away with Cartland?"

"I was thinking that one out, Manson. But why should she go back to the house? What was on the table? The prepared meal, and the afternoon-delivered mail—his private mail since it was delivered to the house."

"Suppose," went on Manson, "suppose they'd planned for Joseph Pevensey to give him the works at the inn? *Then* she went back to clear away the meal so's it'd look as if he'd died of food poisoning contracted at home?"

Knollis did not answer. Manson stared absently through the windscreen.

"No," he said, "that won't do. It was bound to come out that he'd taken tea with her—bound to in a small village like Locksley!"

"I don't know what we'll do," said Knollis. "This case started too easily. I thought we'd be through it within two or three days, and now look at it!"

"You don't think Gabby went back, that she went back to clear up as Mrs. Cartland was away? She has a key."

Manson changed geared and slowed down the car. "We can go back and ask her. And yet why waste time? Didn't she tell us that everything was tidied up for her when she got there next morning? Somebody else must have gone in the house. You're too darned right, Knollis!"

Knollis signed. "Oh, for the touch of a vanished hand!" he quoted.

"Whose hand?"

"Sherlock's. He'd have started at scratch and had this case tied up in two shakes of a lamb's tail. We're mugs beside the detective of fiction, Manson."

"That bloke of yours tries to make you sound like a second Holmes!" Manson retorted.

"Dramatic license", said Knollis.

"It should be endorsed," said Manson. "That makes me wonder how Ignatius is getting on with things!"

"He's solved it," said Knollis. "He said so. I wish I dare take him by the shoulders and shake him until the truth fell out of his mouth."

"I wonder . . ."

"You wonder what?"

"He said he'd give information only if we put an innocent person in jeopardy. He did say that."

"Yes, he said that, Manson."

"Then why not? Why not arrest Morley or the wife? Arrest someone and force his hand. We'll get strips torn off us later, but the end will justify the means. Make him come clean against his own wishes!"

"It would work, Manson, but it wouldn't be ethical. All things are lawful, but not all things are expedient. That's St. Paul."

Manson raised an eyebrow. "You read the Bible?"

"Why not?"

Manson shrugged. "Oh, I don't know. I just—well, I was surprised, that's all."

"Don't expect me to spend all my days reading Hans Gross, Moriarty, and the American comics, do you? Although I must admit I have a liking for Li'l Abner and the Dagwood family. Now Abner's mother, Maw Yokum, would solve this quicker even than Sherlock. She'd knock the truth out of somebody—"

"Which is what I'm suggesting we do with Ignatius!"

"We'll save it as a last resource, Manson. Ignatius is a friend, and I hate working fast ones across friends."

"Funny little bloke, isn't he, Knollis? Protects even a fellow like Davidson."

"Has he converted him, I wonder," mused Knollis.

"Davidson's capable of working something across an innocent like our priest!"

"I didn't mean it that way, Manson. Ignatius isn't innocent, but a clever little man who understands human nature right to the last drop in the barrel. He didn't convert Davidson. What he did was enlighten him regarding economics. He knew Davidson's weak points; a love of money, and a vanity in his complete triumph over locks, bolts, and bars. He exploited his weaknesses and turned them to good account—which is to my mind to more justifiable than the normal mode of conversation, which usually boils down to pushing naked savages into trousers and brassieres—respectively—and teaching 'em how to catch civilized diseases."

He looked round at his companion, but Manson did not appear to be listening. He was apparently driving in a trance. Knollis was thankful that the road was clear.

"I've got it, Knollis!" Manson whispered. "I've blooming well got it! I know who went to the house!"

"Hm?" asked the startled Knollis. "Who?"

"Shardlow and Davidson!"

"Hm-mm! You may have something there . . ."

"Came to me while you were talking," Manson said modestly. "Funny how things come to you like that, isn't it? Did she really go to the theatre, or did she invent that when Morley rang her up about the keys? Did Davidson really go to the night-club? You know his reputation as the Alibi King. Suppose he put a stooge in the club while he took Mrs. Shardlow to Locksley?"

"What for?" asked the doubting Knollis.

"Any further evidence that might help to fetch the mob down. You know Mrs. Shardlow's crusading temper!"

"We haven't disposed of Mrs. Morley yet," Knollis reminded him.

"Neither have we thought of any sensible reason why she should have gone back," Manson protested. "The other two had sound reasons. Davidson was tearing mad for revenge, and Mrs. Shardlow was capable of anything from murder down to house-breaking in the interests she was pursuing."

"From house-breaking to murder," Knollis repeated grimly. "How did they get in?"

"Mrs. Shardlow told us she had duplicate keys to the shop, provided by Davidson. Isn't it likely they had the whole bunch duplicated?"

"Most likely," said Knollis. "How do we prove your idea?"

"Use the old gag. Keep 'em apart, and make each believe the other had talked."

"Mrs. Shardlow wouldn't believe it of Davidson."

"He'd believe it of her after the way she strung him along!"

"I think you're perfectly correct," said Knollis. "And if you're wrong we'll still try it, because we're up a gum tree anyway."

He stuck a cigarette in Manson's mouth, and held his lighter under it. "Somewhere in this case is a remarkably clever person who's hoodwinked us all along the line, Manson. It isn't often I feel despondent about a case . . ."

"It isn't necessarily the strongest motive that wins the prize," said Manson. "Cartland had a good one for doin' in Morley, and the reverse is also true. I don't think Davidson is the murdering type, but you never know with a woman, and as I see it either Mrs. Morley or Mrs. Shardlow were quite capable . . ."

They returned to town, and to the Spaniels. They knew Mrs. Shardlow had not been at the Cartland house, and hoped she had sneaked away to spend an hour with her husband, still virtually confined to barracks at the inn.

"Your wife been in?" Knollis asked as he entered Shardlow's room.

"And gone again, sir," said Shardlow, putting his book aside and standing up.

"Where to?"

Shardlow scratched his head. "I'm not sure, sir. She's got Mrs. Cartland's car, and is supposed to be shopping but she said she'd a spot of detecting to do before she went back to Locksley."

"Not again!" groaned Manson.

"We'd better get in touch with her and tell her to come and say goodbye to you. I'm sending you back—not to Parkhurst though. I'm making arrangements for you to be held at Brixton or the Scrubs *pro tem*. So you don't know where she's gone!

"I haven't a clue, sir."

Knollis and Manson went on to Pirelli's Club to make enquiries. Then they called on Davidson.

"Where were you on the night Cartland died?" Knollis asked brusquely.

"I thought we'd gone into all that," Davidson retorted while he studied his fingers intently.

"We've gone into it twice and had two different stories," said Knollis. "We've called for the latest version. You must have one!"

"I don't know that I have," said Davidson.

"Cut it out," said Knollis. "You were in Locksley!"

"Oh, I see what you mean, Inspector."

"We've called at Pirelli's place, and there was no one in the club that night but established members. Serves me right for not checking your statement, of course, but the result is the same. You were out at Locksley?"

"Yes, suppose I was."

"With Mrs. Shardlow?

Davidson seemed genuinely surprised by the remark. "With Mrs. Shardlow? No, I was alone, Inspector. Mrs. Shardlow was at the theatre—so far as I know, that is."

Knollis thought hard for a minute, and then nodded.

"I want your full programme, Davidson, and all of it this time if you expect your passport to be returned to you."

"There was nothing to it, really," Davidson said airily. "I went to see if there was anything in the house worth bringing away. I was still hankering to square the account with Cartland. Mrs. Shardlow had told me Mrs. Cartland was away, so I banged on the door, and when nobody answered I simply let myself in."

"With what? A jimmy?"

"You know I had duplicates made of Cartland's keys! Mrs. Shardlow told you that. There was a latch key for the front door on the ring, and I kept that one for myself. You never knew what would come in useful in my old trade."

"And then? When you got inside?"

"Oh, well, the usual! I had a good look round, decided there was nothing worth bringing away, another go at the shop, and that was all."

"No, listen," said Knollis. "You know I'm not gunning for you but I'm seeking information about the state of the house. Did you notice anything unusual?"

A slow grin crept over Davidson's aristocratic face. "There was a meal nicely laid out for me!"

"Good lord!" exclaimed Manson. "So that was it! You ate it!"

Davidson nodded. "I was darned hungry. Do you know I had to cut some more bread and find myself some cakes in the pantry?"

"Damn!" said Knollis. He stared angrily at Davidson, and bit deeply into his lip. A private theory had flown out the window.

"The sauce?" he asked sharply. "You took that with the beef?"

"It would have been unappetizing without it, Inspector."

"Any indigestion afterwards?"

Davidson patted his yellow pullover. "A thing I've never suffered from."

He looked steadily at Knollis and Manson for a space and then said: "Are you wondering if the stuff was doped?"

"That was a theory," Knollis said sadly.

"It wasn't, Inspector. It was a very nice meal, and I felt much better for it—especially with a double tot of Cartland's whisky on top of it."

"You washed up?" asked Manson.

"And put the dishes away," said Davidson. He bowed from the waist. "A gentleman always endeavours to assist his hostess."

"Some gentleman," commented Manson.

"Cartland's mail was on the table," said Knollis.

"Yes, it was. I brought it away with me. There was an interesting letter from Farthingale, informing Cartland that Manson urgently desired speech with him, that e was flying up to meet her at the airport, and that Cartland was to keep out of the way. Farthingale would report the meeting later."

"Where's the letter?"

Davidson walked to the drawer and returned with three envelopes. "There's also a bill for garden stuff, and an estimate for a new greenhouse boiler."

Knollis glanced quickly through the letter and handed it to Manson.

"What did you do next, Davidson?"

"Went to Pirelli's place."

"Come off it," said Manson. "You weren't anywhere near the door!"

"Okay!" said Davidson in a resigned tone. "I went to the airport. I had a neat idea for sabotaging Farthingale's kite, but I couldn't get near the thing."

"Just a minute," said Knollis. "You were at Pilgrim Corner at a quarter to nine, weren't you? It would take you twenty minutes to get from there to Locksley even in that speedy little car you own. You looked round the house, washed and cleared away after eating the meal, and then went to the airport? That correct?"

"Correct," Davidson said laconically, chewing on a matchstick.

"Then why didn't you see Cartland's car?"

Davidson switched the matchstick over to the other side of his mouth. "I think I did. I do now think I did."

"Ah!" said Knollis. He sought a chair and lowered himself into it. "Where was it?"

"As I came up the hill from the Vale. The ridge road leads off to the right, and the road to the airport to the left. I did my kerb drill on reaching the cross-roads, looking to right and to left. I saw the rear lights of two cars, one roughly ten yards past the corner on the left of the road. The other was a good way further on, on the right side of the road as I looked along it—"

"That would be Cartland's," interrupted Manson.

"There was somebody walking between the two," went on Davidson; "somebody walking away from the first car towards the second one."

"You took your time crossing or turning, didn't you?" said Knollis.

"Inspector," said Davidson, "the only time I landed in hospital was after crossing a similar intersection with halt signs to right and left of me. The only way to drive safely is by believing every other driver on the road to be a fool."

"And you made no other investigation?" asked Manson.

"Why didn't you tell us this before?" Knollis demanded irritably.

"Would you in my place? I'm trying to get to Canada as soon as I can, not hoping to hang round for months to give evidence in an assize court, thank you!"

"You can't give us any details of the cars?" Manson asked hopefully.

"Super, I can see red lights in the darkness, and I could see a shadowy figure presumed to be a man walking up the road, but my vision is limited. Probably something wrong with my eyes. I must have them seen to some time."

"I'll get you one of these days," said Manson.

"I'm afraid of that," Davidson retorted. "That's why I'm anxious to put several thousand miles between us."

Knollis interposed. "Seen Mrs. Shardlow lately?"

"Half an hour ago, if that helps."

"What did she want?"

Davidson clicked his tongue. "Shall I tell you? Perhaps I'd better do so. She's got a Thing about Morley, you know, a hunch. She says he's innocent, and thinks the pills poisoned Cartland. To prove Morley innocent she wanted me to find an excuse to visit you at your place of business and half-inch a few of those said pills. She was going to get them analysed. Seems she has an uncle in the business. I refused, of course!"

"Of course," said Manson. "You wouldn't do anything dishonest, would you?"

"She's wasting her time," said Knollis. "They've been analysed by one of the best men in the country, and they are harmless indigestion pills."

Davidson shrugged his slim shoulders. "Well, you know what women are like when they get an idea into their heads. You'd better mount a guard over the pills."

"They're safe," said Knollis.

"Inspector," said Davidson.

"Yes?"

"Who did kill Cartland?"

"I think it must have been me," said Knollis. "Everybody else appears to be innocent!"

"Now there's a thing!" exclaimed Davidson. "Wouldn't it make a smashing headline? *Yard man confesses to murder of provincial jeweller*. T'would ring the bells of heaven the wildest peal for years—"

"If parsons lost their senses, and people came to theirs," said Knollis, finishing the quotation for him. "I didn't suspect you of being a reader!"

"I can write with a pen, too," said Davidson. "I'm no moron, Inspector. I read, and I think. I've thought about this case quite a lot, for instance."

"For instance," said Manson, "what conclusions have you reached?"

"I'm afraid it boils down to my late colleague, the pretty Mrs. Shardlow," Davidson replied sadly. "You see, she came up here and got the job with Cartland—heaven knows how she pulled that one! She was here to get her Arthur out of stir—somehow, and she wasn't very particular about her methods, as I know to my sorrow. She knew all about the stuff in the top room at Pilgrim Corner . . ."

"Well? What then?"

"I *did* overhear it said at the police station that he must have taken the dope before he went to meet Morley at the pub."

"That's correct."

"After leaving Morley he went to the shop, and then he drove home. Now suppose Mrs. Shardlow decided to poison him, knowing that if he died at all unnaturally you'd go through the premises with a fine-tooth comb, and find what you did find—"

"Well?"

"That opens the investigation into Cartland's affairs, blows up the gang, and opens the gate to her husband's case?"

"Isn't that exactly what has happened?"

"Of course," said Davidson. "Now suppose she got some dope from the chemist uncle, and put it in some sweets, or chocolate? Or perhaps they had a cup of tea during the mid-afternoon at the shop? See what I mean?"

"Poison in sweets or chocolates," Knollis murmured thoughtfully.

"Nuts!" said Manson with a snort.

"Or nuts," said Davidson, brightly. "A book here says aconite has a bitter taste, but it can be disguised, can't it?"

"Where's the book from?" asked Manson.

"The public library—on a temporary student ticket. Or should I say a student's temporary ticket?"

"Very interested, aren't you?" asked Knollis.

"I'm anxious to be on my way, Inspector. The sooner you crack the case the better I'll like it. And you're stumped, aren't you?"

"Go to blazes," said Knollis, and walked out.

Manson's sergeant met them as they walked the long corridors at headquarters to Manson's office. "Mrs. Shardlow's only just left, Super. She says you'll have to arrange another appointment. She couldn't wait any longer."

"*Another* appointment?" asked a puzzled Manson.

The sergeant looked askance. "Well, sir, she turned up to keep the one with you. I put her in your office—"

Knollis left them, hurriedly. When Manson and the sergeant came up with him he was standing in the middle of the office floor with a tin of pills in his hand.

"—thirty-two, three, four, five, six. Three missing, Manson! We'd better look to our laurels," he said with a broad smile. The Shardlow Private Detective Agency has gone into action. She'll stop at nothing will she?"

CHAPTER XII

THE TRAIL NARROWS

THE THREE MEN stood looking at each other for a few seconds; Knollis smiling broadly, Manson scowling his annoyance, and the sergeant wearing an expression of acute embarrassment.

"You aren't to blame, Phillips," said Manson.

"I should have kept her in the ante room," said Phillips. "I mean, she looks such an innocent and *nice* young woman."

"She is," said Knollis. "She just happens to be in love with her husband, and so like the rest of the sex she has no qualms about reverting to jungle law when the occasion demands."

"Want me to fetch her in, sir?" asked Phillips.

"Doesn't matter now," said Manson.

"You might try to find where she goes," suggested Knollis. "She'll be calling at the Spaniels to see her husband, and you can pick her up there."

"Might be as well," Manson agreed gloomily. "You never know what might come of it. But her action more or less proves she had no hand in Cartland's death!"

"Unless it is an elaborately-planned device to make us believe that."

Manson looked up, startled. "You think she might be capable . . . ?"

"Well," Knollis replied mildly, "that's why I'm putting Phillips on her trail. As you said, you never know what might come of it—and we have to admit we aren't doing too well at the moment."

Manson grunted. "What a heck of a case."

"I wonder who the man was," murmured Knollis.

"You don't think Davidson invented him, do you?"

"No. I think Davidson's getting too worried about his passport to fox us any longer. Now what males have we in the case? There was Cartland himself—"

"Morley."

"Davidson—"

"And that's the lot," said Manson.

"Do note that Davidson *presumed* the figure to be that of a man! So we now need to list the women in the case who own a car."

"The ladies of Locksley."

"Yes, we have Mrs. Morley and Mrs. Cartland. Two only, Manson. The Morley car was supposed to be in dock."

Manson unnecessarily straightened his desk and kept his eyes on it as he remarked: "You know, Knollis, we've taken too many items for granted. I'm having a word with the garage people—when I've found which garage it is."

"Ring Morley, and ask him outright. Shoot the line about doing the final checking of his statements before filing 'em. He'll suspect nothing. He's not remarkably bright."

Manson nodded, lifted the receiver, and asked for the private exchange operator to get Morley on the line for him. He hummed a little tune as he waited, while Knollis gazed thoughtfully at the box of pills which lay beside the telephone.

"Mr. Morley? Superintendent Manson here. We're just doing the final check on your statements before dismissing you from the case. Do you mind giving me the name of the garage you deal with? Doughty's? Thanks a lot."

Then he rang the garage, twice raised his eyebrows at Knollis, and whistled softly as he replaced the handset.

"Got something?" asked Knollis.

"I'll say! Mrs. Morley fetched her car at eight o'clock on Thursday night, and returned it shortly after lunch on Friday, saying the clutch was too fierce. She asked them not to tell her husband she had used it, and tipped the mechanic five bob to keep his mouth shut."

Knollis screwed up his eye and tried to think that one out. "Then where the dickens did she park it that night and next morning?" he demanded. "Morley was at home on Friday morning—we interviewed 'em both at their home."

"This is something!" enthused Manson. "We're getting somewhere now. She's mannish in figure and walk, ain't she? I mean, in the darkness Davidson could easily have mistaken her for a man. There would only be the faint lights from the parking lamps to help him—and if she wore slacks. . . ."

"Don't rush me!" pleaded Knollis. "Eight o'clock you say? Morley and Cartland were still at the Spaniels."

"And Mrs. Cartland at the airport."

"She rang her husband three times that night."

"Who? Mrs. Morley?"

"Who else?" Knollis asked irritably. "She rang him three times. With what object? To make him believe she was at home all the evening?"

"There's a snag," said Manson. "If she was on the road all the time she'd have been bound to use call-boxes, and her husband would know by the noises-off that she was calling from them, and not from home."

"True," admitted Knollis. "Oh, darn the whole case!"

"She might have been reporting to him from time to time. She might have been shadowing somebody."

"Then why bribe the garage bloke to keep his mouth shut?"

"Yes, there is that!"

"How the deuce can we get at her? How the deuce can we find out what she was playing at?" asked Knollis. He began to walk the office floor, beating his right fist into his left palm.

"We could ask her," suggested Manson.

Knollis stopped pacing, and grinned at Manson. "That is really brilliant," he said. "We're getting too het up, aren't we, comrade!"

"Well, do you think it is a workable idea?"

"Of course. Let's go and shatter her into small pieces."

"Don't we do any eating?"

"You can if you like. I can manage until nightfall now we've got this new lead. I like to get out while an idea is hot."

"Oh, well," sighed Manson, "but what about a pint on the way?"

"Not on an empty stomach!"

"A pint, and a plate of bread and cheese," pleaded Manson. "My tummy's beating on my backbone!"

"All right," said Knollis with a smile. "I'll compromise and we'll take ten minutes off on the way there. Know of a good place? As if you didn't!"

"A real nifty little house, The Halfway House. They sell good wallop, and keep good cheese in stock—not rubber substitute supplied on the ration in mouse-trap sizes."

"That's three and a half miles," Knollis said respectively.

"It looks like one inch by one inch to me," said Manson.

"I mean the ruddy distance from here to the pub!"

"No, you're wrong if we're not talking about cheese. It's the halfway house between Burnham and Beddington. If you're in a statistical mood, Burnham is seven miles from Locksley, and Locksley is seven miles from Beddington. You take the right turn to the airport, and then branch left down a slip-road to Beddington. The pub is roughly half a mile on yon side of Locksley village."

"And the beer's good!" said Knollis with a peculiar smile.

"You'll see for yourself."

"I can't get there quick enough," said Knollis.

Manson looked at him suspiciously and led the way to the main entrance and the waiting car.

The snack meal proved to be as appetizing as Manson had prophesied, and Knollis began to realise that he also was hungry. He ordered a second plate of sandwiches, to which he added two slices of fruit cake and a second round of beer.

"Quite all right, gentlemen?" asked the hovering landlord.

"Very tasty," said Knollis. "We must call again."

The landlord was turning away when Knollis said: "Let me see, was it Thursday, or Friday, when my friend Mrs. Morley left her car here all night?"

"Eh!" exclaimed Manson. "Heck!"

"Oh, Mrs. Morley recommended you, did she, sir?" said the landlord. "Why, it was Thursday night—the night Mr. Cartland came to his rum end."

"You did as she asked, and kept quiet about the car being here?" said Knollis.

"Oh, yes, sir. I know Mrs. Morley very well, and I knew it was all above board even if it was a bit queer."

"Do you know my friend?" asked Knollis quietly.

The landlord looked at Manson. "I've seen him somewhere before, sir, but I can't recall his name."

"He is Superintendent Manson of the C.I.D."

"Oh! A detective!"

"I'm another," said Knollis laconically, "only I come from New Scotland Yard."

"We're investigating Cartland's murder," said Manson. "Curious business, wasn't it."

"Very queer sir," said the landlord, eyeing him more cautiously now.

"What story did Mrs. Morley pitch you?" asked Manson.

"Pitch me, sir?"

Knollis interposed. "The Super is asking what excuse she offered when she asked you not to let anyone know the car was here all night."

"She said she'd fetched it from the garage in town without Mr. Morley knowing, and she'd done some damage and wanted to get it put right before he found out. She said she'd have to crawl in third gear to get back because she'd stripped the top gear. She took it into town just after lunch on Friday."

"That will be all," said Knollis.

Manson paid the bill a few minutes later, but in the meantime remained silent, watching Knollis curiously.

"How the deuce did you know she'd left it here?" he asked when they were once more on their way.

"I thought it out," Knollis said modestly. "I couldn't imagine her parking it with any of her friends. It wasn't left in the open, or in any of the woods, or your blokes would have found it when they went to work. She couldn't have left it in any old barn or disused farm building for the same reason. She couldn't have parked it in Cartland's double garage, or Davidson would have seen it and remarked on it—he would, you know, if only as a further stunt to save his own skin."

"You really do detect, and think!" said Manson with un-grudging admiration.

"You know your *modus operandi* rules," said Knollis, ignoring the compliment. "If a bloke does a job in a way that succeeds the first time, he then tends to do all other jobs by the same method. Mrs. Morley, as I reasoned, had already tried it when she bribed the garage bloke. There is some confusion, I'll admit, as to whether she bribed him when taking it out or taking it in, but the reasoning was fairly sound in either case. When you told me where the pub was situated, I said to myself: *That's the place.*"

"It's a good job Morley didn't call at the garage to see if the car was ready," commented Manson. "He might easily have done that when Cartland let him down by not calling for him. He'd be stooging round the shop, getting fed up with waiting, and it was quite on the cards for him to mentally consign Cartland to Hades and hop round to see if the car was available."

"The garage people probably made a practice of phoning a client when his car is ready," suggested Knollis.

"That, or have one of the hands run it round to the shop. Anyway, the main thing is that your discovery gives us something to throw at Mrs. Morley."

Manson slipped his clutch, switched off the engine, and let the car coast down the slope to the Vale. "I wish we'd got Joe Morley either tied up or thrown out of the case," he said miserably. "He can't prove he was at the shop, and we can't prove he was anywhere else!"

"It's the oldest of all alibis, Manson. *I was in bed at the time.* Once a man says that you've a dickens of a job proving he wasn't."

"Hello," said Manson. "Look who's here!"

Knollis glanced up to see Brother Ignatius ambling along the road toward them. "Pull in, Manson. We'd better have a natter with him. He might feel in the mood to throw a few nuts to two poor old monkeys."

Brother Ignatius nodded affably as Knollis stepped from the car. "I see you are following the trail in a duly logical manner, as is your wont, Gordon. I saw your car coming down the hill from the Halfway House. You now know that Mrs. Morley kept her car there on Thursday night. You'll find her at home with a perfectly good story for you."

"The case's lousy with good stories," Knollis said dryly "We've had three from Davidson up to now."

"Davidson is a very silly man," said the little priest. "I asked him to tell you the truth from the very beginning, but he appears to like exercising his creative imagination. The last statement he gave you was, however—"

"The revised version," snorted Manson.

Brother Ignatius flashed a friendly and appreciative smile. "And the authorized version, too, Super."

"Whose car was it he saw on the road that night?" asked Knollis.

The priest took off his wide-brimmed hat and hung it on the radiator cap. "Gordon," he said in the politest of tones, "you are not so thorough as I imagined."

Knollis tipped his own hat to the back of his head. "All right, Ignatius! I am always willing to learn. What have I missed?"

"This is a firm," said Manson. "What have we both missed, Brother?"

"You know the time when Davidson saw the cars on the ridge road?"

"Of course. About half-past nine!" said Manson.

The priest smiled, and considered his pink and well-manicured hands. "You should really ask that of Mrs. Morley. The inn-keeper will corroborate her story. You see, Gordon, there is a perfectly logical answer to every question that may arise from the case."

"I've noticed it," Knollis said facetiously.

Brother Ignatius removed his hat from the radiator and planted it on his head. His re-adjusted his thumb in the fork of his staff, and walked away with no more than a casual nod.

"What d'y'know about that!" demanded Manson.

"I daren't say it," said Knollis. He got back in the car and slammed the door. "Let's have the truth out of her, Manson!"

Kathleen Morley met them with a friendly smile, and invited them indoors. She was wearing a flowered house-coat, and a cigarette was hanging from the corner of her generous and over-rouged lips. She did not appear to be perturbed by their arrival, and was certainly not embarrassed by Knollis's first and very direct question.

"Why didn't I tell you about using the car?" she repeated. "My husband was present."

"What difference did that make?"

"Well," she said easily. "I didn't want him to know where I'd been, or what I'd been doing."

"And what had you been doing, Mrs. Morley?"

"Trailing Roger, of course."

"Trailing Cartland, eh?" murmured Knollis. "Why *of course*?"

"Wasn't that the sensible thing to do considering he'd been here to tea, and I'd threatened him?" she asked.

"Finish the argument, Mrs. Morley," said Knollis.

"I knew he was going to meet Joe, and somehow I could not get Sir Edmund Griffin's talk out of my mind. Roger was very interested in it at the time. You know some of the men went back with Roger for drinks? Joe told me afterwards that Roger pressed Sir Edmund for simply tons of information about murders—and he isn't a reader of detective and crime stories! I should say he wasn't, wouldn't you?"

"Dunno," said Knollis. "Depends where he is now, and what he's doing."

"But you do see what I mean, Inspector?" Mrs. Morley asked lightly.

"You tell us," said Knollis. "We don't like using leading questions."

"Well, I thought Joe would be safe while he was at the Spaniels. It was afterwards I was worried about him. I just did not trust Roger as far as I could see him. I daren't tell Joe of my suspicions because he would have said I was talking rubbish. Joe's a bit literal minded, and thinks anything like that is pure imaginative melodrama.

"I got the car after something of an argument with the mechanic, and I drove to the Spaniels. My car, with me in it, was at the lower end of Spaniel Row when Joe and Roger came out. I followed them to the theatre, and then to the shop. Roger dropped Joe there. They talked for some minutes, and then Roger drove away while Joe walked down Mayflower Street to the shop."

"Where did Cartland make for?"

"The airport. He parked outside the gate as if waiting for someone. He pulled out some minutes later and set out for home."

"Following a taxi?" asked Knollis.

"Following nothing but a very erratic course, Inspector. After a time he settled down to hugging the edge of the road. I decided he was drunk, and I was satisfied that Joe was safe, so I passed him and went home. I came home, telephoned Joe to make some sort of alibi for myself in case he'd rung through while I was out, and got no reply. I ran the car to the Halfway House and parked it for the night. I walked back across the fields, and it was then I heard the shouting and general uproar on the hillside. I carried on past the house, and eventually learned the news about Roger. Then I rang Joe to tell him."

"No one spoke to Cartland while he was waiting at the airport gate?"

"No, I'm sure of that."

"Surely something gave him a reason for going, and then for driving away?" said Knollis.

"There was a man standing by the gate, trying to light a cigarette."

"Didn't he light it?"

"After striking three matches, yes."

"Could you describe him—even sketchily?"

"He was a fat little man. I can't go further than that, except to say he was wearing a trilby hat."

"Which stitches that up!" said Manson. "That was Comrade Farthingale."

"I did wonder," said Mrs. Morley. "The match-striking was a signal?"

"It's extremely likely," said Knollis. "You knew Mrs. Cartland was meeting Farthingale there? It was probably a sign to tell Cartland she'd been, and gone back to town."

Knollis stood with his eyes narrowed to mere slits, staring beyond Kathleen Morley, and apparently through the wall beyond the lounge.

"You got no reply when you rang your husband? You're sure you're telling us the truth, Mrs. Morley? You've made several—shall we say mis-statements?-several mis-statements in the course of these interviews. You're sure you've got no additions or corrections to make?"

"Inspector," she said solemnly, "I've told you the whole truth!"

Knollis heaved a sigh. "All right, Mrs. Morley, I'll accept that assurance. But one final question; your husband was in perfectly good health when he arrived home on Thursday night?"

She gave him a perplexed and puzzled glance. "Yes, perfectly. We've told you that already. He was tired, but then so was I. We'd been losing sleep and worrying over what we were going to do about Roger."

"Thanks," said Knollis.

She showed them out, and stood on the step to watch them down the drive to the car.

"You were correct, I think, Manson," said Knollis. "Joseph Pevensey Morley wouldn't stick round the shop all that time waiting for Cartland He was too jumpy and nervy. If he had stayed he'd have bitten his nails down to his knuckles. Let's have a word with the garage people."

The manager of the city garage was willing to help as much as he could. Yes, Mrs. Morley had certainly taken out the car on the Thursday evening, and put him in a spot when doing so. Her husband came later in the evening for it, and he'd had to shoot the story that it had been taken to the department in the next street for some reason or other. He had lent Morley a car in which to travel home."

"You lent him one?" asked Manson, with a curious glance at the bland Knollis by his side. "At what time?"

"Quarter to nine. Perhaps a bit later. I didn't notice."

"When did he return it?"

"Before lunch on Friday. It would be getting on for twelve o'clock."

"And Mrs. Morley?"

"She brought their own car in during the afternoon, as we've already told you."

Knollis followed Manson from the garage, and they stood on the pavement for some minutes discussing the interview.

"Y'know," said Manson, "I've had a hunch all the way through that Morley was our man!"

"He couldn't do it, Manson—not on the basis of the time-table!" Knollis protested. "We'll say he took out the car at ten to nine. He had to get to the Vale by half-past if he was to push Cartland down the hillside."

"Which is possible," Manson interrupted.

"But he had to drive back to Burnham before his wife rang him to tell him about Cartland! I suggest he left the car—"

Manson waved an impatient hand, cutting Knollis short. "They're in it together," he grunted. "He found out his wife had the car. She rings and gets no answer from Mayflower Street. Both ask awkward questions, and there is a showdown. The rest is sheer collusion! They decided to work together, each pretending the other didn't know what he or she was doing—if you can sort out what I mean. I've suspected it all along!"

"Well, I haven't," Knollis admitted, "but we'll see what we can make of it for you."

"Now let's eat," said Manson.

CHAPTER XIII
VANISHED HOPES

KNOLLIS DID NOT feel like mixing Manson and murder with his meal, so he found an excuse for returning to the Spaniels, and there took a shower while Mrs. Wooderson prepared a meal for him. Shardlow had been taken to London, Mrs. Shardlow had vanished, according to a report which had come into headquarters, and all Knollis had to think about now was the culpability or otherwise of the Morleys, Kathleen and Joseph Pevensey. Even if they were innocent they had acted strangely, and the time was ripe, and more than ripe, for them to give complete and satisfactory explanations of their conduct.

Knollis had know them for a week only, but he was a shrewd judge of human nature and had summed up both husband and wife in a manner that would not have been despised by a professional psychiatrist. Joe Morley was a complete introvert, finding his satisfactions in his own mind, his own home, and his workshop. There was, of course, no such thing as a complete introvert, and encouraged by Cartland he had managed to fit himself into the social round. Nevertheless, he was basically an introvert, and had faced his problems in the manner of a man who must think out each arising situation for himself, reach his own decisions, and be solely responsible for them. Perhaps the one exception in his life had been when his wife and Roger Cartland pushed him out of the shop at Pilgrim Corner and into the one in Mayflower Street.

Faced with Cartland's murder, and the revelations that preceded and succeeded it, he had metaphorically retired to the secret chambers of his own mind, and what he had thought, and what he had decided to do, were nobody's business but his own. Again, he was a negative type, as vacillating as Hamlet himself, and he would find it difficult, if not actually impossible, to take any positive action. In Knollis's opinion he was more inclined to sit in a corner biting his nails and hoping for something to turn up to save him. He had done nothing.

Kathleen Morley was his extreme opposite. She was the complete extravert, and more than something of an exhibitionist. She tended to act melodramatically and impulsively—as when fetching Cartland for tea and reading the Riot Act to him, and later shadowing him in the family car, and, if it came to fine detail, going to the trouble to take down Sir Edmund Griffin's talk verbatim, complete with the questions and answers that followed.

Knollis scrubbed his back vigorously with the bath-brush. What did it all add up to? That if any violent action had been taken by Joe Morley it had been sponsored by his wife, and against his own inclinations. If any similar action had been taken by Kathleen Morley it had been on her own initiative, and it wasn't likely that even her own husband had been taken into her confidences.

Knollis sluiced and dried himself, slipped into his dressing gown and slippers and went back to his room. He dressed slowly, still turning the case over in his mind. Where had Morley gone with the borrowed car? And what had happened to Cartland after Mrs. Morley decided to pass him and make for home? Knollis did not believe in coincidence, and so it would have been silly to believe that Cartland had picked up a casual lift and been murdered by him. Such things did happen, but not in this Cartland case!

Somebody, very obviously, must have been waiting for Cartland. Who knew he was going to the airport? Farthingale and Mrs. Morley. *Unless somebody else had followed him, waiting an opportunity.* But who, known to be concerned with the case, was likely to do that No, it boiled down to Farthingale and Mrs. Morley! Could it have been Farthingale after all—the hitherto unsuspected person? Could the match-striking have been a signal for Cartland to move off, to await Farthingale in some remote spot away from the airport and curious eyes. There was no absolute solid evidence, but there was reason to believe that Farthingale had not moved very far from the bar of the smoke room in the airport hotel. Hang it! It must have been Kathleen Morley!

Knollis rolled up his dressing-gown and threw it across the room. The whole thing was impossible! It was no light task for a woman to steer and push a car and passenger across a rough grass verge, through a gap in the wall, and down a rough slope covered with bracken.

There were two main problems to be solved. Who administered the aconite that killed Cartland? Who pushed him down the hillside? Was one person responsible for both actions? And

138 | FRANCIS VIVIAN

that did not seen possible. The people who were in his company during the daylight hours had alibis for the hours of darkness. The people who might have been with him on the ridge road—his wife, Mrs. Morley, and Davidson—could not have been with him at the approximate time, when, according to Robins, the poison was fed to him.

A knock sounded on the door, and Knollis called: "Come in!"

Mr. Wooderson pushed open the door and introduced Sergeant Phillips into the room. The landlord apologised for interrupting and reminded Knollis that a hot meal was waiting for him in the Crusader room.

"Bring drinks for us," said Knollis, "and the sergeant can talk while I'm eating."

Mr. Wooderson went downstairs, and Knollis and Phillips went along the heavily-carpetted corridor to the Crusader Room. A roaring fire was burning in the grate, and Knollis grimaced as he saw that Mrs. Wooderson had laid the table so that his back would be towards it as he ate. He moved his plate and cutlery to the opposite side of the table, and motioned to Phillips to sit on his right.

Phillips opened his mouth to begin his report, and paused when he saw Knollis staring queerly at the table.

"So that was it!" he said.

He said no more until Mr. Wooderson arrived with his tray.

"Now was this table laid when Cartland and Morley dined here last Thursday evening?" he asked.

"As it is now, Inspector. You get the best light on the table that way. I see you've moved. The fire was too hot on your back?"

Knollis nodded, dismissed him, and asked Phillips what news he brought.

"You'll smile, sir," said Phillips. "I finally trailed Mrs. Shardlow to Sir Edmund Griffin's house up at Willow Leas. She was there about twenty minutes, and then drove back to Locksley Vale, to Mrs. Cartland's."

Knollis did smile. "That's funny," he said. "Going to our own expert to prove us wrong! But what's this story about Mrs. Shardlow vanishing?"

"I wouldn't say she's vanished, sir," said Phillips. "One of the blokes was busy in the village, and saw her come from the house with two suitcases to a waiting taxi. He took the taxi number, checked later, and learned that the driver saw her on the London train from Victoria Station."

Knollis nodded. "Gone back home now her husband's been returned to the south. Nothing to it. Anyway, she'll be satisfied that our experts are really experts and not mugs. Fancy going to see Sir Edmund! That really is funny."

Phillips emptied his glass, and said he would get back to headquarters.

"Ask Superintendent Manson to get the Morleys in for questioning," said Knollis. "If he isn't in, see to it yourself, please. I'll be down in an hour's time."

The grilling of the Morleys was not a long proceeding, but it was a thorough one.

"We usually interview vital witnesses alone," said Knollis, propping his elbows on Manson's desk and making a temple of his fingers. "We are making an exception in your case—"

"We like you, you see!" Manson said sarcastically. "You have been so helpful to us!"

"We are making an exception in your case," Knollis repeated, "for reasons of our own."

"And if we don't get the right answers we shall provided you with board and lodgings," said Manson.

"But we've told you all we know!" protested Kathleen Morley.

Knollis ignored her, and looked direct at Joe Morley.

"Where did you go in your car borrowed from Doughty's garage? You took it out at a quarter to nine, or perhaps ten minutes to nine, and returned it on Friday morning. Where did you go?

"I followed Mrs. Cartland."

Knollis grimaced. He had not thought of that possibility, and saw he was going to make a fool of himself unless he was very careful.

"From where did you follow Mrs. Cartland?" he asked.

"Pilgrim Corner. After Roger dropped me I went to the shop, looked around to make sure all was secure, and then walked up and down the service lane trying to think what could be done about Cartland. I was turning at my gate to walk back when I saw a woman come into the lane from St. Giles's Lane. There's a lamp round the corner, and I saw her silhouetted against the glow. I was certain it was Mrs. Cartland, although I was sure Kathleen had said she was going to Wainfleet that day. She seemed to vanish all at once. I went to the rear of Cartland's premises, and listened. She was opening the back door."

He broke off to ask if he could smoke. Knollis nodded. As the two Morleys lit their cigarettes Joe Morley went on:

"I walked into St. Giles's Lane, and couldn't see a car parked there, so I went round the corner into the Square and looked down Mayflower Street. There was a stationary car on the opposite side, and about twenty yards away. I walked to it, and recognized it as Mrs. Cartland's. My garage is round the corner, so I went for the car. It wasn't ready, so I borrowed one, and drove into Mayflower Street. She came out, looked cautiously around, got into the car, and drove off. I followed her about five miles, and came back to town when it became obvious that she was making for the main road and possibly on to Wainfleet."

"What did you do with the car?"

"There's an empty provisions dealer's shop lower down the street than my place and I used the old garage at the back. I thought it would look a bit silly taking it back the same night."

"Then you really went home by bus?" Can you prove that, Mr. Morley?"

Morley produced a ticket from his ticket pocket, and got up to push it across the desk. "That's the exchange for my return ticket."

Knollis silently handed it to Phillips, who took it and left the office.

""You've no more tickets, Mr. Morley?"

Morley shook his head. "I haven't done a bus journey home for months, Inspector. On the odd occasions when the car has gone wrong, or Kathleen needed it, I've got lifts both ways with Cartland—just as I was expecting last Thursday night."

"Suppose Cartland had returned for you?"

Morley grinned. "I couldn't have told him I'd been following his wife, so I should have said I'd dropped into the little pub in St. Giles's Lane for a short one."

"Logical," nodded Knollis. "You didn't see a man loafing in the service lane, or thereabouts?"

"No. Just Mrs. Cartland."

"He would probably be prowling round while you were in the garage," said Knollis. "Anyway, it may relieve you to know that practically all you've told us has been confirmed by another witness."

Morley blew a sigh of relief. "Then you've finished suspecting us! You're really satisfied that we'd nothing to do with Roger's death? It's been awful—detectives calling at the shop, detectives calling at the house, and detectives round the village. I never want to go through it again!"

Knollis sat like a sphinx, no expression on his face, but his eyes fixed thoughtfully on Morley's blue eyes and red hair.

"We're satisfied that you had no part in Cartland's death," he said, "But we aren't sure about your wife."

"Inspector!"

"But I—I—" stammered Kathleen Morley.

"You've done some funny things," said Knollis, "and by funny I don't mean humorous. Why, for instance, did you go to the trouble to report Sir Edmund's talk verbatim?"

"I told you that!" she protested. "I wanted all the detail I could lay hands on for my crime stories!"

"There are plenty of good books about the Yard," countered Knollis. "Both Richard Harrison and Stanley Firmin had written excellent ones within the past eighteen months. You can find Moriarty, and Gregg, and Sir Basil Thompson's works in the libraries, together with the best works on toxicology and jurisprudence—Glaister, Glaser, Trench, Dixon Mann and Brend . . ."

"Oh, I know," she replied irritably, "but it isn't like getting it straight from the horse's mouth!"

"I doubt Sir Edmund would appreciate being described as a horse," said Knollis. "Still, we'll accept the explanation, but was it necessary to go gallivanting all over the countryside in your husband's car?"

"She didn't," said Morley.

"I'm afraid I did, Joe," Kathleen Morley said softly. "I was so afraid that Roger might try to kill you some way or another, so I fetched the car from the garage and followed you both from the Spaniels. I parked the car with Ledenham for the night."

Phillips returned, nodding to Knollis and Manson.

"Okay! The ticket was issued last Thursday night, and exchanged Friday morning. And there's Mrs. Cartland outside, asking to see you. She's carrying a large zip-up bag and seems in a bit of a sweat. She says it is vitally important that she sees you immediately."

"Stay here with Mr. and Mrs. Morley," said Knollis. "We'd better see her, Manson."

They found Mrs. Cartland in Superintendent Lawton's office, agitatedly explaining that she now knew who had poisoned her dear Roger.

"If I had known who she was earlier I should have known it couldn't possibly have been anyone else," she said tearfully. She bit her lip to stem the tears, and went on: "She was the friend of that Davidson man, wasn't she?"

"No," said Knollis as he closed the door. "She was the wife of Police-constable Shardlow, who's been doing time for a framed country-house robbery which was organised by your husband and brother, Mrs. Cartland."

"My brother? William—as well as Roger?"

"Partners, Mrs. Cartland," Knollis explained briefly. "What is this new evidence you've got for us?"

She swayed a moment, pulled herself together, and wrenched a dead Rhode Island Red hen from the bag.

"Mis—Mrs. Shardlow fed the hens for me after she got back from town today. Most of them are now dead, and the others are dying. This is one of them."

"Heck!" said Manson.

Knollis appeared to be unmoved.

"Then she went to her room and stayed there. The window overlooks the poultry yard at the side of the house, and behind the big yew hedge. Later she came down and rang for a taxi. She had been weeping. She refused to speak to me. When the taxi came she brought her luggage down, and was driven away. It was afterwards that I found the poultry . . ."

"Have the Morleys sent home," Knollis said wearily. "The case is finished. Thanks, Mrs. Cartland! Thanks very much!"

He walked out slowly, followed by two very curious and puzzled superintendents.

"Who's the culprit, Knollis?" asked Lawton.

"I don't know. I doubt if we shall ever know now. You can tell the C.C. I'm going back to town in the morning. I'm beaten for the first time in eleven years."

Manson and Lawton glanced uneasily at each other.

"There must be a solution, and there must be a way of getting at it!" Manson said angrily.

"Look at things squarely and objectively, Manson," said Knollis. "The Morleys couldn't have done him in. Neither could Mrs. Cartland, nor Davidson, nor Farthingale, nor—"

"Mrs. Shardlow could, and did," said Manson, almost shouting his desperation.

"She could, but she didn't," said Knollis. "The motive is twisted the way you're looking at it. Don't you see she was trying to get herself and her husband back in the clear? Trying to get him re-instated in the Force—and not trying to get herself hanged. She's a policeman's wife, Manson, a woman knowing a good deal of procedure and the way we work on these cases. She wanted her husband back in uniform, and Cartland and his band of not so merry men in quod, not herself swinging at the end of one of Teddy Jessop's hemp ropes! Look at the thing, Manson! Look at it squarely! There's no good done by mere wishful thinking!"

"Then we've had it?" asked Lawton.

"You've had it," said Knollis. "I'm going to have an early night and a good sleep."

"I won't sleep," said Manson. "I haven't had a decent night's sleep since we interviewed that batty maid in Locksley! It's like when you get a tune in your head and can't get rid of it—don't the psycho blokes call it cerebral perseverance? All day long and all night long I get it! *Postie brought packet for Mis'Car'land! Postie brought packet for Mis'Car'land! Postie brought packet for Mis'Car'land . . ."*

"You're slowly going crackers!" said Lawton.

"Not so slowly!" said Knollis as he slammed the door behind him.

CHAPTER XIV
OUT OF THE BLUE

THE BLUE LIGHT filtering through the flowered curtains was soothing, as was the soft humming of the lace machines, but Knollis could not sleep. Each time he dozed a picture superimposed itself on his mind, that of a long dark country road with two cars standing on it, and a man walking between them in the lights of the parking lamps of the hinder one. And, to his annoyance, the music of the lace machines now had words which were repeated over and over again like an ancient chant: *Postie brought packet for Mis'Car'land! Postie brought packet for Mis'Car'land! Postie brought packet for Mis'Car'land!*

"Oh, be damned to this!" snorted Knollis. He got out of bed, pulled on his dressing-gown, found his slippers, and went down the stairs to the Woodersons' domestic quarters. He knocked on the door and opened it. "Sorry to disturb you," he said. "I can't sleep! Do you happen to have a cup of tea lying idle?"

"We soon can have," said Mrs. Wooderson. "We never need any more than one excuse to brew tea at this house."

"Come and sit by the fire," said Wooderson. "You're overtired, you know, Inspector. You look all in. Like a spot of what-goes-down-warm in your tea? Yes, I think it's called for!"

He fetched a bottle of whisky from the bar, while Mrs. Wooderson filled and switched on the electric kettle.

"Things not so good?" asked Mr. Wooderson.

"Things couldn't be any worse," sighed Knollis. "We've closed the case—beaten by what must be the cleverest man or woman in all England!"

Mr. Wooderson said "Oh!" and relapsed into silence. The tea was brewed, and cups poured out, and the whisky was tipped into two of them liberally. Knollis drank his cup, had it refilled, and began to nod before the blazing fire.

Postie brought it! Postie brought packet for Mis'Car'land.

Mr. Wooderson was saying something about Sir Edmund Griffin having honoured the house with his presence during the day. "A very clever man, Inspector!"

Postie brought it! Postie brought packet for Mis'Car'land!

Knollis opened his eyes with a start. "My God!" he ejaculated. "And I nearly missed it! Mrs. Wooderson, will you please fill me a flask of tea? Mr. Wooderson, will you get my car from the garage?"

"Something occurred to you?" Mr. Wooderson asked lamely.

"Only the solution to the case!" said Knollis. He almost ran through to the telephone, and as Mr. Wooderson went out to the yard and the garages he heard Knollis announcing who he was and demanding to be put through to the Leicester C.I.D. on the instant. It was half-past eleven when he left the Spaniels, and it was a weary and travel-soiled Knollis who re-appeared at the Spaniels at half-past eight next morning.

"Successful, Inspector?" Mr. Wooderson asked as he almost automatically filled and switched on the kettle. "Another tenner for the hangmen, eh?"

"No, this is one of those cases where justice will have to be left to God, Mr. Wooderson."

"Ah, well," said Mr. Wooderson, "He probably knows better than most of the judges and jury."

Knollis worked his way through a good breakfast of cereal, bacon and egg and sausages, and toast and marmalade. Then he shaved and washed without hurrying, and at a few minutes to ten got into the car and drove to Willow Leas.

Sir Edmund Griffin saw him from the library window, and came to the door to meet him.

"Good morning, Knollis! Nice to see you, but what brings you on this cold morning?"

"I've called to say goodbye," said Knollis.

"You look a wee bit grim, a little more Knollis-like than usual. How is the case progressing?"

"Solved," said Knollis.

Sir Edmund closed the door and led the way into the library, the door of which he also closed. He poured two glasses of whisky, pushed the tray with the water and soda towards Knollis, and waved him to a seat. "You must tell me all about it, and, of course, in the classical term, whodunit!"

"Ever heard of enteric pills, Sir Edmund?"

Sir Edmund laughed. "Why, of course!"

"How are they made and what is their purpose?"

"Well now, an ordinary pill is made by rolling the medicament in gelatin and then coating it with sugar. An enteric pill is also coated with gelatin, but the pill is then dipped in formalin, which hardens the gelatin. An enteric pill, you see, is made to pass through the stomach and be dissolved in the intestines."

"That factor could cause a grave error of judgement to be made by an inexperienced doctor?" suggested Knollis.

Sir Edmund leaned back in his chair and smiled benignly over his rimless glasses. The morning light made his hair look like spun silver.

"What are you trying to say is this, Knollis; that if an experienced doctor examined the body of a man who had died of aconite poisoning he might well declare that he had taken the poison, but, say, an hour before?"

"Quite," said Knollis.

"Whereas, if aconite was incorporated in enteric pills, the truth would be that the man might have taken them two hours—or even three—before death."

There was a break in the conversation while Brother Ignatius was shown into the room.

"Help yourself, and make yourself at home, Ignatius! Knollis and I are discussing enteric pills."

"I wondered if you might be," said the priest as he officiated at the whisky bottle and decanter.

"Knollis has solved the Cartland case, Ignatius," said Sir Edmund.

"I thought that might be the case," said the priest. "Pray do not let my presence interrupt the conversation. I shall be a most interested listener."

"Usually, in these murder affairs," said Knollis, "we work backwards from effect to cause. In this instance we are working from cause to effect. There was a person who hated Cartland a great deal. He also hated Farthingale and everything he stood for. Gauging the psychology of the average detective quite well—if not quite accurately—he made a murder plan which would also expose Cartland, Farthingale, and all who had been connected with him."

"Obvious, surely!" remarked Sir Edmund. "But I see you are leading up to a point, and so I must not disturb the train of your thought."

"Six months ago the person began dealing with a firm of medical herbalists in Leicester by post—in the name of the housekeeper," said Knollis.

Brother Ignatius wandered round the room as Knollis was talking, and finally chose to lean against the door in a most negligent and unpriest-like attitude, one hand holding his glass of whisky, the other pushed through the slit of his cassock and into his trouser pocket.

"Now down in the Sussex village of Lonsdale St. Peter's lived a constable and his wife, the Shardlows. Shardlow went to prison for a crime had had not committed, and his wife was determined both to avenge him and clear his name. She had an uncle in the Burnham district, although she had not seen him, or corresponded with him, for a good many years. She appealed to him, and being a man of influence he persuaded certain other Burnham citizens to recommend her services to Roger Cartland. Cartland was innocent in many ways, as most egoists are, and he employed her. She was already working with Gentleman Davidson, each, unknown to the other, using their partner to obtain information which in the language of solicitors was of great advantage to them.

"Now this unknown uncle—"

"Unknown uncle?" murmured Sir Edmund. "But go on!"

"This unknown uncle sat back and watched, and probably decided that the game was not moving fast enough, so he took a hand. He was a chemist, capable of rolling pills; capable, too, of making enteric pills. So that was what he did. He made enteric pills, put them into an eyewash tablet box, used chemicals to delete the type from a letter written by Grove & Meadows, and typed a note purporting to come from them which asked if Cartland would kindly try the enclosed new pills and report on them in due course. He didn't want to go all the way to Leicester to post them, so he took the only risk he allowed himself—and so brought the case to a conclusion."

"This is a most fascinating story, Knollis!" said Sir Edmund Griffin. "I can never be sufficiently grateful to you for taking time out to come and tell me."

"I learned my job at your feet, Sir Edmund," said Knollis. "Your lectures while I was stationed at Burnham were the basis of whatever success I may have achieved."

"Nice of you to say it, Knollis! I deeply appreciate the compliment! Still, you were saying . . ."

"He took the risk of going to Cartland's house to deliver the pills, knowing from his niece that both Cartland and his wife were out. He handed them to Gabby, the part-witted maid."

"A very risky thing to do!" said Sir Edmund. "Why, she might have told Cartland who delivered them!"

"Our man was a good psychologist—or shall we discard the jargon and say he was a knowledgeable student of human nature? He gave the girl a tip, probably more than she had ever owned in her life. Having impressed her with money, he gave her a lesson to repeat as if she was a child at school. It sounds a bit like an old chant. *Postie brought packet for Mis' Car'land—* repeat *ad nauseam*."

"Working on the principles of suggestion," nodded Sir Edmund. "He probably realised that she would repeat it to herself until she really believed it, until it actualised itself in her mind. What was the substance of it? That the postman had brought the packet for Mister Cartland? Quite clever, I think! What do you think about it, Ignatius?"

"An inspiration—of the devil," replied the priest.

"There must be more to the story than you have told me, for all that," said Sir Edmund. "Loose ends that need tieing and trimming off.

Knollis emptied his glass and slid it on the table. He got to his feet, and thrust his hands deep into the pockets of his grey tweed jacket. "I'm in need of one fact only—the identity of Mrs. Shardlow's uncle."

"That still remains unknown?" said Sir Edmund. "How frustrating for you! Perhaps Ignatius can help."

"Perhaps he can, and perhaps he cannot," said Knollis. "I'm not going to ask him."

Sir Edmund got up, and the two men faced each other across the room. "How much longer does the play continue, Knollis? When do we reach the climax, the startling *denouément* demanded by all the best audiences? And I'm sure Ignatius makes a most appreciative audience!"

"The play is over," said Knollis. "You murdered Roger Cartland, Sir Edmund!"

Sir Edmund smiled. "Arrest me, Knollis! Warn me that anything I may say will be taken down in writing and may be produced in evidence! Haul me before the magistrates, have me committed to the assizes! Have your case put before twelve good men and mentally incompetent!"

Knollis shook his head. "You've got me, Sir Edmund! I know exactly what happened—and I can't prove it. I've been to Leicester during the night, and dragged the director of Grove & Meadows out of bed. He's shown me the list of Burnhamites the firm supply by post. Your name isn't on the list, but your housekeeper's name is. You had the run of the forensic laboratories until a fortnight ago, although you had retired. You could roll pills and bleach notepaper to your heart's content. Nobody can prove you were on the Locksley Road last Thursday night, but I know you were there. We can put Gabby Jones in the witness box, and the defense will prove that it has been as easy for us to put our story into her head as it was for you to coach her in repeating that the postie brought the package for Mister Cartland!"

Sir Edmund stroked his silver hair, and smiled paternally. "My dear Knollis! My poor dear Inspector Knollis!"

He sighed. "This is a silly story, and one I do not wish to listen to any longer, so you will excuse me?"

He walked to the door and turned the handle. Then he looked down. "Where's the key?"

Brother Ignatius threw it across the room to Knollis, who caught it and pocketed it. "Thanks, Ignatius. I do want to finish the story before I leave."

"I pity you," said Sir Edmund. "I really pity you, Knollis! This is your first failure in a major case in eleven years. The great I-Am is beaten at last! How the Sunday newspapers will play up the story! My poor dear Knollis!"

He poured himself a second glass of whisky, and raised it to his lips, which wore a mocking smile.

"You know, Knollis," he said, "when we come to look at life we have to admit that there is only one thing we really value—all of us with the exception perhaps of our dear brother here. The good opinion of the rest of the world! *Vanity of vanities! All is vanity.*"

He looked deep into Knollis's lean face and asked: "Why are you smiling? Surely you have nothing to smile about! Knollis! Why *are* you smiling?"

"As always, Sir Edmund, I can learn from you, right to the very end!"

Sir Edmund put down his glass and walked across the room to face Knollis, his hands on his hips with the thumbs in the front. "You mean . . ."

"When I get back to Burnham," Knollis said slowly and significantly, "I shall hold a press conference. I shall admit that the case has gone bad on me, and is closed. I shall explain that in the early stages I submitted a box of pills to Sir Edmund Griffin, the noted forensic expert, for analysis. He failed to find aconite in them, whereas a member of a famous firm of medical herbalists . . ."

"Knollis," Sir Edmund said sharply. "You can't do this to me!"

"The great I-Am," Knollis said contemptuously. "The reputed forensic expert who could not analyse a simple pill! We'll see whose reputation suffers most."

Sir Edmund took a turn round the room and came back to Knollis's feet. "Knollis! I can't have that! You understand? I can't have it! I'll give you a complete confession, witnessed by Ignatius. I'll stand my trial—"

"You darn well will not!" said Knollis. "Have you standing there in the dock as the cleverest murderer of all time, Sir Edmund? Not on your life!"

"It isn't legal, Knollis!" Sir Edmund almost shouted. "You will be an accessory after the fact. You will become a partner with me. You will be equally responsible, Knollis. For the sake of our friendship in the past, please accept my offer. I *will* give you a full and complete confession. Please . . ."

"You can go to your master—the devil," said Knollis.

"Your conscience, Knollis! Remember the oath you swore when you joined the Force!"

"That is a matter of importance to myself alone," said Knollis. "I'll wrestle with my conscience in my own way and in my own time."

Sir Edmund sank into the nearest chair and covered his face with this hands. "And I was writing my life story," he said in a broken voice.

Knollis walked to the door and unlocked it. "I'll wait in the car for five minutes, Ignatius, in case you'd like a lift back to town."

Ignatius touched him gently on the sleeve. "You are really going through with it, Gordon?"

"Yes, Ignatius, I am."

"So be it," said the priest. "God works through us in strange and mysterious ways. I will join you in a few minutes."

* * *

Three days later Knollis and Brother Ignatius faced each other across a table in the restaurant in Bridge Street. Between them lay the morning paper. At the head of the centre column of the front page was a photograph of the late Sir Edmund Griffin, described as England's Foremost Forensic Expert.

"Food poisoning," murmured Knollis. "Well, that was perhaps the only solution!"

"You had him in suspense," said Brother Ignatius. "He would never have been quite sure whether you would destroy his reputation or not, and it looks as if he preferred to leave this life with his reputation intact."

"I feel like a hangman," Knollis said wryly.

"Why more so than if you had provided the evidence justifying his hanging at the hands of Mr. Edward Jessop?"

"Teddy Jessop's paid for the job."

"So are you—indirectly," said Brother Ignatius. "We are all responsible for Griffin's death, whether he was hanged or committed suicide. *Society* is responsible, Gordon, and that means you and I."

Knollis sniffed, and refused to be comforted.

"What finally put you on the right track?" asked Brother Ignatius, anxious to steer Knollis's mind into more practical channels.

"Mrs. Shardlow's peculiar actions. I learned that she'd stolen some of the pills from Manson's office and was taking them to be analysed. I learned she had an uncle who was a chemist. I then learned that she's been to see Griffin and that struck me as humorous. Then Mrs. Cartland turned up with her story and the dead hen. She said Mrs. Shardlow had avoided her, and refused to be drawn into conversation—and regarded it as a certain sign of her guilt. As I drove back through the night from Leicester I realised the truth, that Griffin was her uncle, and that she's been *ashamed* to face Mrs. Cartland because she knew that he'd murdered Roger Cartland."

Brother Ignatius sighed, and rolled the tablecloth up from its edge and let if fall again like a roller-blind. "I had certain advantages which were not granted to you—one of the doubtful benefits of my vocation. I realised from the onset that Sir Edmund's infamous lecture to the ladies of Locksley was deliberately intended to put ideas into the heads of Morley and Cartland, and quite seriously speaking I don't think Sir Edmund would have cared which of the two was murdered providing the death caused the eventual exposure of the gang. He was, as you rightly surmised, a vain man, and smarting under the sting of the many tricks they had played on him. But the game went slower than he anticipated, and he decided to take the active part. Once I realised that I set to work, thinking my way logically, step by step, through the case."

"My solutions came through intuitive hunches," Knollis said dryly.

"Paradoxical," murmured the little priest. "Still, that is life all the way through."

"Let's have a drink," said Knollis brusquely. "What shall it be?"

Brother Ignatius pondered. "Perhaps inappropriate to the meal, but Lachryma Christi, I think."

"The tears of Christ," said Knollis. "Yes, you're right, Ignatius. You know, I still feel a sneaking sympathy with old Griffin."

"Naturally," smiled Brother Ignatius, "for with him your vanity has taken a really considerable kick in the pants—if I may descend to the vernacular."

He sat back in his chair and chuckled. "It will do you good."

Knollis cast a curious glance at him and remained silent until the wine was served. Then, with a wry smile on his lean face he raised his glass. "To Brother Juniper!"

"Yes, to Brother Juniper!" said Brother Ignatius.

THE END

Lightning Source UK Ltd.
Milton Keynes UK
UKHW021454250319
339847UK00006B/194/P

9 781912 574438